B is for Bella

A story from the village of Sixpenny Cross
~ Inspired by Life ~

Victoria Twead

New York Times and Wall Street Journal bestselling author of the internationally acclaimed *Old Fools* series.

Copyright © Text, Victoria Twead, 2016
Copyright © Cover painting, Nick Saltmer, 2016

Published by Ant Press, 2016
First Edition

The author asserts the moral right under the Copyright, Designs and Patents Act 1988 to be identified as the author of this work.

All rights reserved. No part of this publication may be reproduced, stored in a retrieval system, or transmitted, in any form or by any means without the prior written consent of the author, nor be otherwise circulated in any form of binding or cover other than that in which it is published and without a similar condition being imposed on the subsequent purchaser.

Also available in Large Print and Digital editions

Contents

Chapter One	5
Chapter Two	6
Chapter Three	11
Chapter Four	17
Chapter Five	24
Chapter Six	29
Chapter Seven	36
Chapter Eight	41
Chapter Nine	47
Chapter Ten	54
Chapter Eleven	59
Chapter Twelve	64
Chapter Thirteen	70
Chapter Fourteen	76
Chapter Fifteen	82
Chapter Sixteen	90
Chapter Seventeen	96
Chapter Eighteen	101
Chapter Nineteen	106
Chapter Twenty	112
June Tait's Cinnamon Hazelnut Biscotti	114
Also by Victoria Twead	116
Chickens, Mules and Two Old Fools	120
Contact the Author and Links	121

Chapter One

When I was younger, I used to amuse myself in the evenings by sewing patchwork quilts. That quilt you are sleeping under now was made for your mother. Sometimes I blink when I see you curled up in that crib because you, my dear, are the spitting image of her.

Now I have arthritis in my hands, and I can scarcely hold a needle in my crooked fingers. My poor old eyes can't see the stitches either, so I'll sew no more patchwork quilts. Heaven allowing, I'll teach you, little one, when you're older.

My own mother used to make patchwork quilts, as did her mother before her. Our quilts were washed so often that they became faded and threadbare. But we never threw them away, even when holes began to appear.

No.

Everybody knew who would be grateful for them.

Bella Tait.

Sweet Bella Tait couldn't bear to see any animal in need and cared for so many creatures that she needed all the old towels, quilts and bedding she could lay her hands on.

B is for Bella.

I'll tell you the rather unusual story of Bella Tait while you sleep, little one. It'll keep my mind busy, now that I have no quilting projects on my lap.

You see, Bella Tait and Christine Dayton were born within weeks of each other. And though they were almost neighbours, they were *never* friends.

Chapter Two

In the heart of Sixpenny Woods is a curious rock. Nobody knows how old it is, or how it got there. Some say it's made of granite, but there are no traces of natural granite in that part of Dorset. How and why that huge rock came to be resting in the woods is a mystery.

Plenty of guesses have been hazarded. Some suggest that it is the remnant of some giant rock that struck our planet countless years ago. Some say it was transported by Druids, to serve as an altar. Others whisper that aliens were responsible for the appearance of a rock so out of character with its surroundings. Gypsies camp around the rock, believing in its magical qualities.

Whatever their opinions, most agree that the rock possesses supernatural powers, and since time immemorial, the inhabitants of Sixpenny Cross have called it the Wishing Rock.

The rock is nearly as tall as some of the trees around it. It is weathered and smooth, with little holes and crevices, inviting one to climb it. Ivy fights to take hold, its tendrils creeping over the surface.

In 1954, Bill Haley & His Comets recorded *Rock Around the Clock,* and Roger Bannister ran the first under four minute mile in Oxford.

That same year, a married couple were enjoying a Sunday walk through the dappled light of Sixpenny Woods.

"Hey, I'd forgotten all about the Wishing Rock!"

exclaimed the young man, running up to it and pulling away the ivy to reveal the dark stone beneath. "Why don't we climb it?"

"Don't be silly, Don, it's far too hot for climbing. You climb it if you want to."

"Oh, come on! We should climb it and sit on the top, then we can both make wishes."

"Knowing me, I'll fall and break a leg."

"No, you won't, I'll help you."

They scrambled up and sat close together on the narrow summit, legs dangling. Don draped an arm around his wife's shoulders. The trees were green, thick and silent around them.

"Go on, then. Make a wish," said Don.

"You know what I'm going to wish for," June answered, a faraway look in her eyes.

"Yes, I do, but don't tell me or your wish won't come true."

June squeezed her eyes shut.

Please, Wishing Rock, no more miscarriages, no more stillbirths. Let me have a healthy baby. I don't mind what it's like, a boy or a girl, fat or thin, ugly or pretty... Just one healthy child.

Beside her, Don was also wishing.

Please help me to take June to Italy to see her grandmother's village. I'd give my life to see her exploring the place where her family came from.

On the other side of Sixpenny Cross, another husband and wife stayed indoors, oblivious to the beautiful day and the sunshine streaming through their dirty windows.

"You stupid woman! You're pregnant again? For gawd's sake, what do we need another brat for?" The man leaned forward, eyes narrowed to slits, his finger stabbing her shoulder. "Get rid of it! Did you 'ear me? I said *get rid of it.*"

His wife stared at him as he emptied a beer bottle down his throat.

Maybe I will get rid of this one, she thought bitterly.

He belched.

Or maybe I won't. That would teach Mr 'igh and Mighty.

She raised her own beer to her lips and drank deeply.

bbbbb

Months passed. It was April the 5th, 1955, and Britain was shocked, but not surprised, to hear the following radio announcement.

The Right Honorable Sir Winston Churchill had an audience with the Queen this evening and tendered his resignation as Prime Minister and First Lord of the Treasury, which Her Majesty was graciously pleased to accept.

The man who had led Britain throughout the war was eighty years old and his health was failing.

Down in the south of England, in the Tait household in the village of Sixpenny Cross, nobody heard the announcement. The radio wasn't even switched on.

A new life was beginning. And from the second that June and Donald Tait's newborn baby took her first gasp of air and yelled, she was adored.

"It's a girl!" said the midwife. "A beautiful baby girl with an excellent set of lungs. Let me just give her a little wash, and then I'll pass her to you and call your husband upstairs before he wears out the linoleum with his pacing up and down."

June lay exhausted but numb with happiness. After all

the miscarriages and two heartbreaking stillbirths, they finally had a perfect, healthy baby.

"Do you know what you're going to call her?" asked the midwife.

"Yes. She'll be named Bella. After my Italian grandmother. Bella means 'beautiful' in Italian, you know."

"A lovely name," said the midwife. "A beautiful name for a beautiful baby."

To be fair, only a midwife or the baby's parents would have described this baby as beautiful. Little Bella's face was scarlet, screwed up and furious.

Donald had heard the cry and didn't need calling; he raced up the stairs and charged into the bedroom. Standing at his wife's side, he clutched her hand.

"Is the baby okay?" he asked the midwife.

"Bless you, she's perfect! Here you are, I've wrapped her up. Meet your brand new little daughter."

Oh so carefully, Donald took the precious bundle from the midwife and sat down slowly on the edge of the bed. He gazed at his daughter's angry little red face, her toothless mouth wide open in a howl.

"Hello Bella," he whispered, "I'm your daddy. How beautiful you are! Believe me, whatever you want or need, for the rest of my life, I'll move heaven and earth to get it for you."

Baby Bella stopped crying and fell asleep. The midwife smiled.

bbbbb

On the other side of Sixpenny Cross, another baby was crying. The man slurped the last of his beer and dropped the bottle on the floor.

"Oh, for gawd's sake shut that brat up!"

"I can't help it if she cries all the time," his wife

protested. "I 'aven't got time to see to her every minute."

"I told you, you shouldn't have 'ad it."

"Too late now."

"Well, call Mary then. I swear if that brat don't stop bawlin', I'm outta here."

"Mary! Mary! Go and see what your baby sister wants, I'm tryin' to get your dad's dinner ready."

"But Mum, why does it always 'ave to be me?"

"Because I said so. Rock the pram a bit, see if she'll go to sleep. If she doesn't, dip 'er dummy in a drop of your dad's whiskey. Then just shut the door on 'er so we don't 'ave to listen to her bawling. And get me another bottle of stout from the cellar when you've done that. I'm parched."

Mary stamped out and they heard her speaking to the baby.

"For gawd's sake, what's the matter with you? Why are you always crying? When I'm older, I ain't going to 'ave kids, they're too much work. And I ain't going to live in Sixpenny Cross. I'd rather be back in Yewbridge, this place is a dump!"

She rocked the pram for a while, but the baby didn't stop crying.

Chapter Three

"Perhaps you'd like to pass her back to your wife and we'll see if Bella will take her first feed?"

June Tait smiled into her husband's eyes and took her baby daughter, holding her close. Still half asleep, Bella latched on immediately and the room fell silent as everyone watched her suckle.

"Well, she certainly likes her food!" laughed the midwife.

That was true, and Bella never lost her love of food. When she was tiny, June and Donald marvelled at her appetite but delighted in giving her the food she so enjoyed. If anything upset her, they'd placate her with a slice of pizza or a few spoons of homemade *gelato*. She was a smiling baby who grew into a chubby, happy toddler, enveloped in the adoration of her parents.

Bella loved everything and everybody. If anybody asked her what she loved most, food and animals came high on the list. Only her parents topped them.

One day, when June was cooking macaroni in the kitchen, Bella toddled outside into the backyard. June caught sight of her daughter through the window. She was squatting on the path.

"Donald, are you there? Bella is in the garden doing something. Could you check on her, please, and bring her in? I'm just about to serve the macaroni."

Donald strolled outside and crouched down beside his little daughter.

"What are you doing, *la mia bella* Bella?"

"Worm!" said Bella, holding up a large, wriggling earthworm for her father to admire.

Donald recoiled a fraction, then smiled at his earnest little daughter.

"Oh! He's a beauty, isn't he? Shall we put him down and go inside and have some macaroni?"

"No!"

"Willy the worm likes to dig in the garden. He doesn't want to be inside with us."

To his consternation, the little girl burst into tears.

"Want worm, want worm!"

Donald thought quickly.

"Don't cry, *la mia bella* Bella. I'll tell you what, we'll find a jam jar. We can fill it with soil and put Willy the worm in there, and take him inside to watch us eat our dinner."

The tears stopped, and serious brown eyes regarded him.

"Well, *la mia bella* Bella, what do think? Shall we do that?"

The little girl nodded.

Father and daughter found a suitable jar in the shed. Donald punched holes in the lid and together they filled the jar with soil.

"Pop him in then," said Donald, and Bella dropped the worm into the jar.

Donald sprinkled some more soil on top, screwed the lid on tight, and the pair returned to the kitchen, just as June was pouring homemade tomato and basil sauce over the steaming macaroni. They put Willy the worm on the counter to watch them eat.

Later, Willy came with them to the bathroom to see Bella have her bath. Willy listened to the bedtime story that June read to her daughter, and he stayed on the shelf when

Donald turned off the light.

"I'm not sure about Bella keeping a worm in a jar," said June later. "It might not survive and Bella will be so upset."

"I can fix that," said Donald.

He took an old shoelace from the kitchen junk drawer and snipped it to roughly the same length as Willy. Then he tiptoed into his sleeping daughter's room, collected Willy's jar and emptied the contents into the garden, giving Willy back his freedom.

Then he refilled the jar with soil, dropped in the shoelace, and added more soil.

When Bella woke up in the morning, her first thought was for Willy.

"Mummy, where's Willy?"

"He's in the jar, darling. He's dug right down but you can still see a little bit of him if you look carefully. He can see you, too. Do you want to bring him to the table to watch you eat breakfast?"

For the next few weeks, 'Willy' went everywhere with the little girl, and she never suspected that she was carrying part of a shoelace around.

Willy the worm was the first of Bella's pets but by no means the last. By her fourth birthday, she was the proud owner of several guinea pigs, two hamsters, a budgerigar and five white mice.

It was only a matter of time before she asked for a kitten, but actually, the kitten found her.

bbbbb

Visitors who drove through Sixpenny Cross couldn't help but admire the village green and the cottages with their neat front gardens. In summer, window boxes were crammed with scarlet geraniums, and the Dew Drop Inn was decorated with hanging baskets stuffed with multi-coloured petunias.

These visitors probably wouldn't have noticed one particular street at the edge of the village. Springfield Road was a cul-de-sac flanked by new redbrick semi-detached council houses. Each one was identical in structure to the next. Some were well cared for, others not so much.

The villagers had fought Yewbridge Council when it was announced that these homes were to be built, and that the new residents would be 'difficult' families rehoused from Yewbridge council estates. But to no avail. The houses were completed and the 'problem' families moved in.

At the police station, PC Arthur Cooper groaned when he heard the news. He was close to retirement and looking forward to the day when he could hand over all duties to his son, Stan, who was following in his father's footsteps.

"Let's hope these new families don't bring trouble with them," he said to his wife.

Arthur changed the route of his beat to take in Springfield Road, just in case. He decided that a police presence couldn't do any harm.

To be fair, the new families hadn't really caused any problems yet. When Arthur cycled up the street every day, some of the residents even greeted him. But already the front gardens looked untidy, particularly the Dayton family's. The grass was overgrown and weed-filled. An old fridge lay on its side, and broken toys and a threadbare sofa sat in the drive.

Young Christine Dayton was often around. Arthur guessed that she'd been told to play outside, and he smiled at her. She stared at him, her ratty little face devoid of expression. Then she poked her tongue out, and turned her back on him.

Charming, thought Arthur and pedalled away.

He didn't see what Christine was doing. She'd found a green cricket in the long grass, and she was pulling its legs off, one by one.

bbbbb

The Tait's cottage in Sixpenny Cross was quite near the village green. One afternoon, June and four-year-old Bella walked over to the pond to feed the ducks. On their way home, Bella tugged at her mother's hand.

"What's that?" she asked, pointing at something in the gutter.

"Oh no," said June. "Don't look. I do believe it's a tiny kitten. I think it must have been hit by a car."

Bella froze, wide-eyed, then burst into tears.

"We have to help it!"

"I think it's too late, darling," said her mother. "I don't think it's alive."

Before June could stop her, Bella wrenched her chubby hand out of her mother's and crouched down. She lifted the mangled body of the kitten out of the dirt. A green eye cracked opened and gazed at her.

"Mummy! We have to help it!"

June jumped into action. She tugged the knitted woollen hat from her head and held it out.

"Quick, put it in there, that'll keep it warm. We'll go home and ask Daddy to take us to the Animal Hospital in Yewbridge."

Mother and daughter raced home, trying hard not to jolt the kitten nestled in the hat.

"Daddy! Daddy!"

"What's the matter, *la mia bella* Bella?"

"We got a kitty wot's been in a accident!"

The urgency in his daughter's voice stopped him correcting her English.

"We have to take it to the hostibal!"

Donald peered at the scrap of fur in his wife's hat and

immediately grabbed his car keys.

"Quick, I don't think we have any time to waste."

Donald's car ate the few miles to Yewbridge in record time. They ran into the building and were immediately attended to by one of the vets. She carefully lifted the broken little body out of the hat.

"Please make her better," begged Bella.

"The vet will do her best, *la mia bella* Bella," said her father, "but that's a very sick kitten."

"I think you should go home," said the vet. "Leave her with me. I'll take a good look at her, and then I'll phone you."

The Tait family left their details at the desk and drove home.

"What will be, will be," said June.

Chapter Four

Later that evening, June tucked her daughter into bed.

"You know the kitty is very poorly, don't you?" she said, stroking her daughter's head.

Bella nodded, a giant tear squeezing from the corner of her dark eye.

"The hostibal will make her better."

"The hospital will do the very best they can. Now snuggle down, and we'll know more in the morning."

A little later, the phone rang.

"Hello, it's Sandra, the vet at the Animal Hospital. I have good and bad news for you," she said. "Your kitten is seriously injured. She has two broken legs and was concussed. The good news is that she has no internal injuries. I think we can fix her, but it'll be very expensive."

She named a figure and June gasped. They agreed that June should first talk with Donald and then get back to the hospital quickly with a decision.

"We can't afford this," said June sadly.

"I know," replied Donald, "but how can we allow the poor little thing to be put down? Bella will be devastated."

"Do we have the money?"

Donald took his wife's hand and gazed into her face.

"You know our Italy money? We could use that."

June looked back at her husband and finally nodded her head.

"Yes, let's use the Italy money."

The Taits had been putting aside a little money

whenever they could. June's dream was to visit Italy and see the village where her grandmother had been born and raised. She wanted to feel the same sunshine that had warmed her grandmother's face, and smell the same Italian scents. She wanted to see the sapphire-blue Ionian sea, and taste the grapes and olives, just as her grandmother had.

It was hard saving up the money for the holiday. Donald didn't earn very much as a mechanic and it wasn't the first time they'd needed to raid the Italy fund. A couple of years ago, the stairs in their cottage had needed re-carpeting. Another time they had to replace the engine in the car.

This time they dipped into it for the sake of their beloved little daughter and a kitten they'd never seen before that afternoon.

"We'll get to Italy one day," promised Donald, and June nodded.

"Who knows?" she said. "Perhaps some day we'll win the football pools."

It was a nice dream.

"*La mia bella* Bella, we have good news for you," said Donald the next morning. "The hospital is going to make your kitten better."

The smile on Bella's face was worth every penny of the Italy fund.

"Can we go and see my kitty?"

"Not today, but soon."

"I'm going to call her Hattie, because she was in Mummy's hat."

"That's a perfect name, Bella. When we visit her, we'll tell her."

Bella beamed, and her parents basked in her happiness.
At Yewbridge Animal Hospital, Donald and June were worried that the metalwork on the kitten's tiny legs might alarm Bella.

Nothing could be further from the truth. Bella was fascinated by the hospital and the treatment. Years later, Donald and June agreed that visit to Yewbridge Animal Hospital marked the day that little Bella Tait decided her future.

The vet was patient, taking time to explain in simple terms why Hattie had metal pins in her back leg, and how the splint and plaster cast on her front leg would keep the bone straight while it healed.

"When you take Hattie home, you'll need to keep her in a little crate. She mustn't move around much. It's very important that she keeps as still as possible while her legs mend."

Bella absorbed the vet's words and nodded.

At last they were allowed to take Hattie home, and Bella took on most of the nursing duties. She fed the kitten by hand, and stroked her head until she purred. She sat with her, making sure she wasn't lonely and didn't move too much.

When Hattie's treatment was over, she was as lively and agile as any kitten could be. Apart from a slight limp, she was as good as new.

"Mum, can I 'ave some money?"

"What for?"

"Sweets."

"What d'you think I am? Made of bloomin' money?"

"It's not fair!" Christine kicked the wall in temper.

"I'll tell you what I *will* give you, though. A smack round the chops, that's what I'll give you."

Her hand shot out. The slap was sharp and spiteful.

Christine gasped. But she didn't cry.

Bella's first day at the village school in Sixpenny Cross was harrowing for both mother and daughter.

When the school bell rang, they followed the other mothers and children inside. Bella's new school uniform swamped her, and her leather satchel and lace-up shoes squeaked with newness.

Another mother dragged her daughter into the cloakroom. The child was thin and pasty, with a ratty face and small, hard eyes like marbles that stared at the world defiantly. Her school uniform was crumpled, stained and clearly secondhand.

"Christine, get a move on," snapped the mother. "I 'aven't got all day."

June and Bella found the peg labelled 'Bella Tait' in the cloakroom. Christine Dayton's peg was next to it.

"Right, so 'ere's your peg," said Christine's mother, hanging her daughter's coat on it. "Now, I'm off. Get yourself into the classroom, and *behave*. I don't want to 'ear no stories from your teacher that you been playin' 'er up."

Christine said nothing and showed no emotion on her pale, pinched face. Flat eyes stared at Bella and her mother. She didn't even say goodbye to the departing figure of her own mother.

June was finding it hard to leave.

"I have to go, darling," she said at last, gently detaching Bella's arms from around her legs. "I'll pick you up later, and we'll have spaghetti for dinner, shall we?"

Bella wasn't used to other children or the noise. She wanted to be home with her mother and Hattie and all the animals. She opened her mouth and howled. Christine Dayton stared on in fascination.

"Hello Bella," said the teacher, crouching down to her level. "Mummy will be back to pick you up this afternoon. Now, I wonder if you could do something for me? Our goldfish needs feeding. Can you help? And then after that, do you think you could draw me a picture of all your family?"

Bella stopped crying.

Christine needed no consoling. She flitted from one activity to the next, quickly tiring of each before moving on. If another child had what she wanted, she snatched it away or pushed them off. Christine's name was the one that the teacher used the most.

"Christine, dear, we don't push each other like that."

"Christine, please don't do that, you could hurt somebody."

"Christine, wait for your turn."

But Christine pleased herself. She stopped to watch Bella hard at work on her picture. She picked up a paintbrush, dipped it into a paint pot and deliberately swiped it across Bella's picture. The blue paint ran down Bella's picture, saturating the paper.

Christine waited, expecting a reaction, but although Bella stared at the blue paint, she didn't complain.

Christine clenched her fists. Bella was supposed to cry. Christine wandered off to cause trouble elsewhere, but she kept looking over her shoulder at Bella.

A little later, the teacher went to see how Bella was getting on with her picture. Bella was still working hard, oblivious to the children milling around her, her tongue clenched between her teeth in concentration.

"You've been busy," her teacher said. "What a lovely picture and what a lovely blue sky. Tell me who you've drawn."

So Bella explained about her mother and father, Willy the worm, Hattie the cat with the limp, the rabbits, guinea pigs, mice, rats and budgerigars.

"Gosh," said her teacher. "What a lot of animals you have! When you've finished that beautiful picture, do you think you could sort out the box of farm animals for me?"

Bella nodded.

"Then tomorrow, we're going to make animals out of plasticine."

Bella rarely cried at school again.

When the mayor of Yewbridge visited Sixpenny Cross village school, he toured the classrooms. He was ushered into Bella and Christine's class, and smiled at the children. Christine Dayton narrowed her eyes, already aware that this was an authority figure, the type of person her parents had taught her to hate. Bella was standing close by, fascinated by the important visitor with the shiny gold mayoral chain around his neck.

"Hello, little girl," he said, patting Bella on the head and ignoring Christine. "Would you like to be a mayor when you grow up?"

"No thank you," said Bella. "I'm going to be a vet."

Nobody was surprised.

Sometimes it seemed as though the Tait family was dogged by bad luck. It was always a struggle to pay the mortgage on the cottage, but other events occurred over the years, each one making it necessary to raid the Italy fund again and again.

"We'll get there one day," Donald said to his wife when their ancient boiler broke down and no amount of tinkering would fix it.

"I know," smiled June sadly, "but we need to buy a new boiler first, there's no question about that. Italy will have to wait."

"Well, I've just filled out this week's football coupon. Perhaps we'll get lucky this time and win the pools!"

But bad luck was always waiting around the corner.

With Bella at school, June took on a part-time job which certainly helped bolster the family finances. For a few hours a week, she helped Jayne Fairweather in the village shop and Post Office, and the Italy fund slowly began to swell again.

"Oh, I can almost smell the lemon groves," said June as she helped Jayne stack cereal packets on the shelf. "And I can imagine the sea, with little boats bobbing about. My grandmother came from a fishing village, you know."

"It sounds just wonderful," said Jayne, leaving to answer the phone.

She came back white-faced. June straightened up and stared at her.

"Jayne? Whatever's the matter?"

Chapter Five

Jayne Fairweather reached out and grabbed June's hand. "It's Yewbridge Hospital. They want to speak to you about Donald."

The colour drained from June's face. She flew to the telephone. She heard a woman's voice answer when she spoke into the receiver.

"Am I speaking to Mrs Tait?"

"Yes," June replied, her heart pounding.

"This is Sister MacArdle at Yewbridge Hospital. Your husband, Donald, had an accident at work but it's nothing to be alarmed about. A car he was working under fell on him and broke his leg. We're putting his leg in plaster before sending him home."

June breathed a huge sigh of relief. It could so easily have been a lot worse than just a broken leg.

An ambulance brought Donald home when his leg had been set in plaster. The hospital lent him a wheelchair and a pair of crutches. Bella was the first to scrawl her name on her father's cast, and then set to work drawing all the animals in the house.

"Does your leg hurt, Daddy?"

"No, *la mia bella* Bella, it doesn't hurt now, but it feels a bit itchy. They showed me the x-ray, and it was quite a clean break. They made sure that the bones were in the correct position, then they set it in plaster to stop it moving about."

"Just like Hattie's cast?" Bella was fascinated by

anything medical."

"Exactly like Hattie's cast."

"Will you have a limp like Hattie?"

"I don't think so. But I'm going to have to stay at home for a long time. I can't go to work until the cast comes off."

Bella was delighted and didn't catch the worry in her father's eyes. Seeing more of her father was very good news. But Donald knew no work meant no pay, and life was going to be tough for a while, even if they claimed unemployment benefits.

As father and daughter chatted, they didn't see the small, pale face hovering at the window, spying on them.

Donald's leg didn't heal well, and weeks, then months, passed and the bills piled up. Once again, June and Donald were forced to dip into the Italy fund.

*****

Christine couldn't remember her father ever having a job. She knew he got something called 'Benefits' and she knew that their money came from 'the Social'.

"Mary, and you, Christine, if anybody ever asks about your dad's back, you tell 'em it's really bad," their mother frequently told them.

"Why?" asked Christine. "Dad ain't even got a bad back, 'as he?"

"'Course he has! That's why he can't work. If the Social don't believe us, we'll lose our benefits. So you make sure you tell 'em about how bad his back is."

So their father continued to loaf around the house, usually with a beer in his hand. He rarely went out, unless it was to the pub.

Christine, young as she was, was left to her own devices. Bored, she discovered she could sneak out of the house and go wherever she pleased. Nobody noticed her absence and nobody ever missed her.

Small for her age, and light on her feet, she developed the knack of blending into the shadows, unseen and unheard. She peeped into homes, spied on her father drinking in the Dew Drop Inn, and watched the vicar through the vicarage windows.

But most of all, Christine watched Bella Tait and her family.

And the more she stared through the windows of Bella's cottage, the more her eyes narrowed and her heart hardened.

Eventually, Bella's father was pronounced fit and he returned to work. Both he and June sighed with relief, as it meant he was earning again.

Around that time, Bella found a tiny fledgling in the garden. She knew that one should never interfere with fledglings because their parents were usually close by, feeding them and teaching them how to fend for themselves.

Bella shut Hattie into the house, and watched from a distance. No parent bird turned up and the tiny fledgling didn't move. Occasionally it cheeped, and its beak gaped, but no mother came to feed it.

Bella approached it, but the baby bird didn't hop away. She stooped down and carefully picked it up.

"Oh, you poor little thing! You've got a broken leg!"

It was so light in her hand she felt nothing at all except the tiny beating heart.

"Don't be frightened," she said, "I know exactly what to do. Hattie had a broken leg, and so did Daddy. We have to make sure your leg is very straight, then put on a splint to keep it like that until it mends."

She took the little bird inside and showed it to her mother. Together they made a miniature splint from a matchstick, but it was Bella's deft, confident fingers that straightened the leg, applied the splint and fixed it in place with sticky tape.

She had successfully treated her first patient.

"Good job, *la mia bella* Bella!" said her father, admiring her handiwork. "Good job!"

Christine, at the window, watched and her hands balled into fists.

bbbbb

Christine hardly heard the shouting matches between her mother and father any more. They happened so frequently, they were almost a nightly affair. It often ended with her mother being slapped about. But that's what husbands did, didn't they? Then her father would collapse into his favourite chair in front of the TV, a bottle of beer at his elbow, and shout abuse at her mother who was preparing his dinner in the kitchen.

But one particular night it ended differently.

Her father swayed up their path, then hammered on the front door with his fist.

"Where are you, woman?" he bawled, "let me in!"

"Eh, 'old your horses! You're 'ome early, ain't you? Did you drink the Dew Drop dry?" asked her mother, opening the door.

"Woman, you won't believe what's 'appened," he said, standing unsteadily over her in the hallway.

"What?"

"They barred me! I ain't allowed to drink in there no more!"

"Really?"

"Yes, really. They've barred me from the Dew Drop!"

"Well, perhaps that ain't such a bad thing…"

Upstairs, the listening child held her breath. It wasn't wise to cross her father when he came back from the pub. Everybody knew that. Booze always made him angry. Christine crept out of her bedroom, knelt down and peered through the bannister at her parents below.

"*What* did you say?" he asked, menace in his voice.

"I just meant we'd 'ave more money perhaps if…"

"*What?*"

"I just meant that you don't need to go to the pub every night…"

But her mother had gone too far.

Her husband's hands were already balled. He swung back and slammed a hard fist into her stomach. Christine heard a little "ouf" as her mother exhaled and crumpled into a pile on the floor, her head hitting the hall stand as she went down.

"You stupid woman," he slurred, kicking her unconscious body. "I ain't staying around 'ere. I should 'ave stayed in Yewbridge. This place is like a bleedin' morgue."

He slammed the front door behind him and staggered back down their path.

It was the last time Christine saw her father in Sixpenny Cross.

Chapter Six

Christine's stomach was growling. She was hungry, and there was nothing in the pantry. Her sister, Mary, was out somewhere, and her mother was snoring on the couch, her mouth hanging open.

"Mum! Wake up, I'm hungry! Can I go and buy some bread?"

Her mother slowly opened her eyes and groped for the cigarettes next to the overflowing ashtray. Coughing, she pulled one out of the pack and stuck it between her lips, reaching for the matchbox with a shaking hand.

"I need money to buy some food," said Christine.

"Do you think I'm made of money? For gawd's sake, we ain't got any, and that's that. You can blame your stinking father for leaving us."

She blew a smoke ring into the air and closed her eyes. As Christine left the room, she heard the glug of liquid being poured into a glass. Her mother was on the sherry again, and there was no point talking to her when she was drunk.

Christine's stomach growled again.

I'll just have to do what I usually do. Steal some food.

It was easy really. Nobody in the village of Sixpenny Cross locked their back doors. All Christine had to do was watch and wait until a kitchen was empty, then she'd sneak in and help herself to whatever was on the table or in the fridge.

She almost drooled at the memory of the pie she had

stolen from the pub pantry, and the freshly baked scones she'd snatched from the policeman's house. Haha! Very satisfying stealing from the police. And it was very funny when the policeman's wife blamed first her husband, and then blamed Stan, their grown up son.

Christine knew where she was guaranteed to find food.

Bella Tait's house! Mrs Tait is always cooking that Italian stuff for Fat Belly Bella and 'er dad. No wonder Bella's so fat! Why, I'd be doing her a favour if I stole some of Bella's food!

The row of terraced cottages that Bella lived in backed onto fields. Hugging the hedges, Christine made her way towards Bella's cottage, then hopped over the low fence. Success. She entered the backyard, crept past Donald's shed and up to the kitchen window. Even before she peeped inside, the delicious cooking smells made her stomach flip.

The kitchen was brightly lit, and June Tait hummed to herself as she drained spaghetti. She gave the sauce a final stir with a wooden spoon. Steam and the scent of herbs and tomatoes filled the little kitchen.

"Don, Bella, tea's ready! Sit up, I'm bringing it in."

She heaped steaming spaghetti onto three plates, then spooned the sauce over.

"Tut, tut, I've made too much again," she muttered and carried the laden tray out of the kitchen to her waiting family.

Christine quietly opened the back door and let herself in. There was plenty of spaghetti and sauce left. All she had to do was help herself. Quickly. She grabbed a bowl from the side and began ladling spaghetti.

"Christine?"

Christine spun round, hunger gnawing at her insides, furious at being caught.

Bella's eyes flicked from Christine to the food.

"Here," she whispered, "use this plastic bowl, it won't

be missed. Take as much as you like, but hurry up!"

"Bella, did you find the parmesan?" June's voice sailed in from the next room. "It's just on the side."

"Got it!"

Bella and Christine evacuated the kitchen at the same time, Bella with the parmesan, Christine with her spoils. She closed the back door quietly behind her.

As she sat in the bus shelter, using her fingers to devour the delicious food, she seethed with embarrassment. She was mortified that Bella, of all people, had not only caught her stealing, but had given her food.

Who did that fat Bella think she was? Miss 'igh and Mighty would probably snitch on her, tell her parents, which meant another visit from that stupid policeman.

But Bella didn't breathe a word about Christine's clandestine visit to her parents, or anybody else.

Was Christine grateful?

She was not.

Instead, the humiliation of being discovered by Bella festered in her soul. If she disliked Bella before, she *hated* her now.

Why should Bella have everything? It's so unfair!

"I'm going to teach that fat lump a lesson," she vowed.

"Miss, my mum put a piece of chocolate cake in my satchel, and now it's gone. I saw Bella eating chocolate cake at break time, I bet she was eating mine."

The teacher looked at Christine in surprise.

"Are you sure?"

"Oh yes, Miss, quite sure."

"Bella, come here a minute," called the teacher, beckoning to Bella who was busily working at her desk. "Did you take some cake out of Christine's satchel?"

Bella's mouth dropped open in astonishment. She stared at Christine, who refused to make eye contact. There was a long pause before she spoke.

"I'm sorry, Miss. I'm sorry, Christine. I shouldn't have taken it, and I won't do it again."

If Bella thought she was doing Christine a favour, she was mistaken. Christine ground her teeth and redoubled her efforts to make Bella's life difficult.

If Bella's homework was lost, or her pencils broken, or her work messy, Christine was usually responsible. But Bella never retaliated or complained.

bbbbb

England went crazy when their team won the football World Cup in 1966. That year the Beatles released their album, *Revolver,* and both Bella and Christine celebrated their eleventh birthdays. It was time to move on from the homely environment of Sixpenny Cross village school.

Bella had done well. The teachers were kind, and the classes small, so Bella felt secure. She didn't make friends easily, but that didn't concern her. She was content with just her father, mother and her pets.

Next term she'd catch the bus to Yewbridge High School, with the other Sixpenny Cross kids. But today had been the last day at the village school and she bid her sad farewells.

"Goodbye, Bella," said her teacher, handing over her end of term report. "Good luck at Yewbridge High."

"I'm so proud of you, *la mia bella* Bella," said her father when he read the report. "With results like these, you'll be accepted into a university to train as a vet one day."

Bella radiated happiness.

That evening, June served one of Bella's favourite

dishes, homemade ravioli, as a treat to celebrate her school report. Bella had three helpings.

In the council house on Springfield Road, Christine tore open the brown envelope containing her school report. She scowled as she read it.

Huh! It was her worst report yet, but it didn't matter. Her mother would never think to ask for it, so she'd never see it. Christine was accustomed to forging her mother's signature. No problem.

*****

That September, when school began again, everything changed.

From inside the Post Office, Jayne Fairweather watched with interest as the kids began to gather at the school bus stop outside. She knew them all.

She saw skinny, defiant little Christine Dayton who lived with her mum and sister in Springfield Road. Christine's mum was a regular visitor to the shop. She cashed in her weekly welfare cheque at the Post Office counter and then spent a good proportion of her money on beer or cheap sherry. Her husband had vanished a long time ago. It was little wonder that young Christine was allowed to run wild. And, if the rumours were to be believed, Christine's big sister, Mary, was pregnant, and had moved back to Yewbridge.

Jayne's favourite was Bella Tait. A sweet child, well-mannered and earnest. A real animal lover, too. Shame that June was such a good cook really, because Bella would be stunning if she wasn't so plump. With that dark Italian skin, brown eyes and glossy black hair, she would be a beauty if she shed a few pounds.

Bella stood a little apart from the other children. She wasn't being unfriendly. If approached, she would have chatted with anyone, but she was shy and unable to join in the easy-going banter of the other children.

The bus appeared and young faces lined the windows, staring down at the waiting children. Bella was nervous. The bus doors swept open and Christine Dayton elbowed her way on first. Then the other children climbed aboard with Bella bringing up the rear.

Jayne waved cheerily but Bella didn't see her. She was on the bus and searching for an empty seat. She found one, sat down, and stared out of the window as the bus drew away.

"Hope Fatty isn't in our class," she heard Christine hiss from the seat behind her.

When they arrived, waiting teachers consulted lists and each student was sent to his or her classroom. Bella and Christine found themselves in the same one.

High School was very different from the village school where she'd been surrounded by children she'd known for years. Here, nearly every face was strange, and where there were never more than sixteen children in a class at Sixpenny Cross, now there were thirty-two. Each time the bell rang, Bella had to change classrooms and found herself amongst more new hostile faces in the corridors.

Unlike Bella, Christine Dayton was quite enjoying High School. It didn't take her long to form a gang, and appoint herself as the leader. Now, when she hurled spite at Bella, her gang was there to applaud her.

"It's Fat Belly Bella!" Christine would crow. "What did you have for breakfast today, an elephant?"

She snorted with laughter and her friends followed suit.

Bella pretended not to hear, and chose a desk as far away from her taunters as possible. She laid out her books and began to study, switching off the conversation around her.

"Fat Belly Bella, will you be goalkeeper when we play

hockey this afternoon? No balls would get past *you!*"

"Hey, Fat Belly, wouldn't like to be near you if you ever explode…"

"Hey, Fat Belly, wouldn't like to be near you if you ever explode…"

The bullying was relentless. Every day there were new insults. A few class-mates tried to put a stop to it, but they were only half-hearted attempts. The truth was that while Bella was the target, the focus was off them. Nobody told the teachers, and they were too busy and overworked to notice.

Physical Education lessons were the worst. Bella had to wear terrible grey shorts and short-sleeved white blouses that accentuated her dimpled flesh, providing additional opportunities for Christine and her gang to torment her. And if ever Bella was in trouble, you could be sure Christine was behind it.

Bella never breathed a word of her troubles to her parents.

"The thing is," she confided to Hattie, her cat, "that if I tell Mum and Dad, it'll really upset them. And if I tell the teachers, I think Christine and her gang will get worse. So I've decided to put up with the bullying and just ignore it if I can."

Hattie purred and rolled onto her back to have her tummy rubbed, all four paws blissfully paddling the air.

Meanwhile, Christine had one aim in her rotten life, and that was to make Bella's life as miserable as possible.

Chapter Seven

"How was school today?" asked June, ladling out a generous helping of pasta onto Bella's plate.

"Good," Bella replied. "We're doing equations in maths, and learning about onomatopoeia in English."

"Oh my!" said June, profoundly impressed and immensely proud of her daughter.

"We're so pleased that you like your new school," said her father, his mouth full of pasta. "But don't you work too hard, *la mia bella* Bella."

Bella smiled at him.

But Bella wasn't the only one keeping a secret. After dinner, when she went up to her bedroom to study, Donald closed the kitchen door and quietened his voice.

"I don't want Bella to hear this. I don't want to worry her."

June sighed. She knew what was coming.

"I'm so sorry, June, but I think we'll need to raid the Italy fund again."

June nodded, resigned.

"For the tax, you mean?"

"Yes. I'm so sorry."

Donald worked as a mechanic but because he was self-employed, he had to file his own tax returns. He'd got himself into a mess this year, and ended up owing the Inland Revenue a large sum of money.

"Of course," said June. "Don't worry, I know we'll get there someday. Italy and my grandmother's village will always be there, waiting for us. When the time is right, we'll go."

<center>bbbbb</center>

When Bella walked into the classroom, she was always prepared to close her ears, duck her head, and quietly make her way to her desk. But today was different. Today she didn't need to. Today Christine Dayton and her gang had found another victim to torment.

"Who set your head on fire?"

Bella quietly sat down, then dared to look up through long lashes.

An unfamiliar boy was standing at the front of the class. His skin was extremely fair, with a generous sprinkling of freckles scattered across his nose. He was very thin, and his shock of red hair stood on end. Bella couldn't help smiling to herself, thinking that he resembled a lit match.

The object of Christine's bullying had flushed a vivid scarlet. Later, Bella would learn that it wasn't fear or embarrassment that caused him to change colour, it was anger.

Their teacher marched in and put her heavy bag down on the desk. The class fell silent.

"Good morning, class. Today we welcome a new boy into our midst. This is Ryan Jenkins. Now, do we have a spare desk anywhere for Ryan?"

"Next to Bella Tait!" Christine shouted, and sniggered.

From anyone else, this may have sounded like a helpful suggestion, but Christine made it sound hostile and unwelcoming.

The teacher ignored Christine and smiled at Bella.

"Is it okay if Ryan sits next to you, Bella?"

Bella nodded, and Ryan picked his way between the desks and sat down.

The teacher began to call out the names in the register and Ryan and Bella stole shy glances at each other. Pale blue eyes fringed by almost white eyelashes looked into deep brown ones, the lashes thick and dark. Each picked up friendly signals. They smiled at each other and knew that they would be friends.

"Hello Ryan, I'm Bella," she whispered.

"I know, the teacher said. Nobody calls me Ryan, I'm Red."

"Hi, Red."

"Hi, Bella. Are you Italian?"

Bella glowed.

"No, but my great-grandmother was Italian. How did you know?"

"Your name, and your looks."

Bella smiled, and Red smiled right back.

"We're doing percentages today, have you done them before?" she asked.

"Yep."

"Good. You can help me."

"*Nessun problema.* No problem."

"Can you speak Italian?"

"No, I just like to pick up odd phrases from different languages, you never know when they may come in useful. You see? That one already did!"

Neither of them noticed Christine watching them, her eyes narrowed, her lips set in a thin line.

Bella and Red sat together whenever they could, happy and relaxed in each other's company. No longer did Bella dread school.

They were a strange couple. Bella's plumpness, olive skin and brown eyes contrasted sharply with Red's bony frame, white skin and pale eyes, all topped with flame-red hair. The pair were teased relentlessly, but they didn't care. Their friendship made them strong and the taunts bounced off.

"Here come Laurel and Hardy," Christine would scoff.

Disappointingly, her jibes had little effect. Anger caused her hands to clench into such tight fists that her fingernails pressed crescent shapes into her palms.

Red was an exceptionally bright student. His photographic memory allowed his brain to take a snapshot of whatever he read, permanently capturing information to regurgitate later. Bella didn't find her studies so easy, but she worked hard, and when she struggled, Red helped.

"You've put the decimal point in the wrong place, that's all," he would say when she'd nearly chewed off the end of her pencil trying to solve a problem.

"Ah, now it works, thanks!"

"*Nessun problema.*"

Red was a natural achiever, but his heart wasn't in it. His school results were good but he didn't enjoy lessons. What Red liked more than anything was working with his hands. It didn't matter what: woodwork, metalwork or later on, helping Bella's father install central heating into their cottage.

Bella and Red became inseparable. At weekends, Red sometimes caught the bus from Yewbridge and came to Sixpenny Cross so that he and Bella could study together. They sat at the dining room table, while June brought them drinks and snacks, and Hattie purred on Bella's lap.

"What does your father do?" Donald asked him one day.

"He's a scientist," Red replied. "He lectures at the university."

"And what do you want to do when you leave school?"
Red sighed.
"That's the trouble," he said. "I'm not like Bella who knows she wants to be a vet. My dad wants me to be a scientist, like him, and work in research or become a lecturer. I don't really want to do either of those things, but I don't know what I *do* want."
"Never mind, you've got plenty of time," said June, bringing in a plate of cake.

Nobody saw Christine Dayton watching through the window. And nobody saw her angrily plucking off the heads of the marigolds in June's flower beds.

Chapter Eight

It was a beautiful day in March. Christine woke late and, bleary-eyed, she stumbled downstairs. She suddenly remembered it was her birthday.

I'm thirteen today!

She hoped that her dad would visit, but that was hardly likely. He hadn't bothered to turn up for any other birthdays, and if he did, her mum wouldn't let him into the house anyway. Chances were he was in prison.

Her sister, Mary, hadn't remembered either, probably too busy with her baby. In fact Christine wasn't even sure her mother had remembered. She found her, as usual, sprawled on the couch, a bottle of sherry close by.

"Mum, it's my birthday, did you get me a present?"

"What do you think I am, made of money? I paid for you to get your ears pierced last month, didn't I? Gawd knows you been nagging me about it enough."

Christine rolled her eyes. Her mother's answer didn't surprise her.

"Right, I'll 'elp meself and party on me own then," she muttered.

She returned to her bedroom and pulled on a pair of jeans and a sweater and planned her next moves.

Downstairs, she stole cigarettes from the pack on the table then raided the fridge, slipping two cans of beer into a bag.

"Just going out for a bit," she called over her shoulder, but expected no response.

The front door slammed behind her and her mood was black as she headed towards the privacy of Sixpenny Woods. Okay, she'd spend her birthday alone. Perhaps she'd climb the Wishing Rock and make a wish. Or maybe carve her initials again into the trunk of a tree. Somehow, gouging living bark with her penknife gave her a sense of satisfaction.

Over the years, the Wishing Rock had lost its battle with the ivy that smothered it. Although the boulder was enormous, it looked like a natural feature, blending in with its surroundings. Unless one knew that it was supposed to possess magical powers to grant wishes, one wouldn't look at it twice.

Christine carefully set her bag on the ground beneath the stone, then began to climb, her hands grabbing at the ivy and her feet seeking out footholds.

At the top, her head was level with high tree branches. She sat down to rest, swinging her legs. She pulled out a cigarette from her pocket and lit it with the lighter she always carried.

Might as well make a wish while I'm 'ere, she thought, inhaling the smoke. *I wish, I wish Bella Tait would find out what it's like to be really miserable, like me. Why should she 'ave everything? I want her to suffer. I don't even care if she dies...*

The delicious notion of Bella Tait suffering gave her renewed energy. She finished her cigarette and climbed down the stone, eager to drink the beer she had stashed. But the cheerfulness didn't last. By the time she'd downed the last drops and hurled the cans into the undergrowth, the blackness had returned. Even carving her initials into a tree only lightened her mood momentarily. It didn't last and her spirits sank to their usual low level. She headed home.

When Christine unlocked the front door, she sensed immediately that something was wrong.

"Mum? Mum? I'm 'ome!"
No reply.
She walked from room to room, but the house was empty. Something caught her eye on the kitchen table. A note.

Sorry Christine im fed up and ive gone away for a bit theres some food in the fridge. make sure you go to scool and Ill see you when I see you. Mum

Christine read the note through three times before she threw it on the table in disgust.
It was the icing on her birthday cake.
Well, she wasn't going to tell the school or the Social that her mum had gone again. If she needed anything before her mum came back, she'd steal it. Easy-peasy, lemon squeezy.
But she couldn't help wondering... How would Bella Tait spend her birthday?

bbbbb

To celebrate Bella's thirteenth birthday, June baked a cake and prepared a birthday tea with crustless sandwiches, *biscotti* and fairy cakes. It was a quiet affair, with just five around the table. Bella didn't want a fuss and apart from Red, and Jayne Fairweather, who was such a good friend that Bella called her 'Auntie', no other guests had been invited.
Christine hadn't been invited, but she was there, nevertheless. Had the Taits or Jayne or Red looked up, they'd have seen her small, angry face at the window. But they didn't, and savoured June's delicious cake and enjoyed each other's company.
In the background, the radio played the English entry

for that year's Eurovision Song Contest, *Congratulations,* by Cliff Richard.

"Congratulations and happy birthday to you, *la mia bella* Bella," said her father smiling. "And here's to many more birthdays."

"I made this for you," said Red, passing Bella a wrapped gift.

"Oh! Whatever is it?"

"Open it and find out," said Red, smiling.

The white face at the window glared at the cosy scene and rolled its eyes.

Bella tore off the paper and revealed an exquisitely constructed small wooden box. It had been lovingly put together using dovetail joints, and then lacquered to a high sheen. But the eye was drawn to the highly decorated oval brass plaque set into the lid. Bella's initials were intertwined with green leaves and pink and white flowers. Tiny, intricate, coloured butterflies settled on delicate petals.

"BMT!" Bella gasped. "Bella Maria Tait! Oh, Red, I love it! Thank you so much, I've never seen anything like that! How did you engrave it so beautifully, and in so many colours?"

"You didn't make that at school, did you?" asked Jayne, admiring the lovely box and running her fingertips over the glossy surface.

"No, I made it at home. I've been tinkering about in my shed," Red explained, "and I made a sort of tool. It isn't perfect yet, but it holds different coloured inks and engraves at the same time."

"That sounds ingenious," said Donald. "You're very clever with your hands, Red."

"I think my box is just beautiful," said Bella, tracing the letters with one fingertip. "Thank you. I shall always keep my treasures in it."

At the window, Christine was incandescent with jealousy. She backed away into the night, passing Donald's car parked in the street. Christine picked up a rock and scored a deep groove in the paintwork, all the way down one side.

bbbbb

The next year, Red made an announcement.
"We're moving," he told Bella, gloomily.
"Where to?" asked Bella, horrified.
"Scotland. Dad's got a job at Aberdeen University. He's really excited about it. Nothing's going to change his mind. We leave at the end of this school term."
"I can't believe it!"
"I can hardly believe it either, but it's true."
"It won't be the same without you." Her eyes misted.
"Bella, we'll always be friends, don't worry."
Bella nodded miserably.
"I'll miss you so much, Red."
"And I'll miss you. But listen, if ever you are in trouble, I will drop everything and come and help you."
"I know. Will you write to me?"
"Of course! *Nessun problema.*"
But it *was* a problem. Red was her best and only friend. Every moment together was precious but the time spent in each other's company evaporated like dewdrops in the morning sun.
A small part of Bella's soul died with Red's departure. She made no attempt to befriend anyone else, but school without Red was dull. Sighing, she threw herself into her studies and worked tirelessly.
Donald and June were concerned.
"You mustn't work too hard, Bella," said her mother, bringing her a plate of chocolate muffins.

"I have to if I'm going to be a vet!" said Bella, chewing.

Christine Dayton left school. Everybody knew she would leave when she turned fifteen, the current legal age, although it would be raised to sixteen in a few years time. In fact, Christine wasn't yet fifteen when she stopped attending school, but the anti-truancy team and teachers didn't fight too hard to bring her back.

Christine's mother eventually returned briefly to the house in Springfield Road. Whether she felt guilty leaving Christine alone in the house or whether she needed to retrieve her welfare benefits was not certain. Rumour had it that she had a new boyfriend in Yewbridge. Soon after, Christine's mother moved back to Yewbridge, taking Christine with her.

A new family moved into the Dayton's house in Springfield Road. The fresh young police constable, Stan Cooper, continued to include Springfield Road on his beat, just as his father had done, but the new family gave him no trouble.

Although Christine no longer lived in Sixpenny Cross, Jayne Fairweather was sure she sometimes caught glimpses of her in the village or lurking in the bushes. Once, when her back was turned, somebody had helped themselves to cash from the till. When she'd looked down the road, she thought she saw Christine Dayton melting into the shadows, but by the time she'd called PC Cooper, the figure had vanished.

That same evening, Donald Tait's car tyres were slashed and Bella's bicycle went missing.

"Who could have done such dreadful things?" asked June, wringing her hands.

Donald shook his head. Bella stared at her feet. She thought she knew who it may have been but she held her tongue.

Chapter Nine

Christine couldn't help herself. She was drawn back to Sixpenny Cross as though by an invisible thread that tugged ever tighter the further she went.

Very early one spring morning, just before the church clock struck two, Christine was back again. She skulked in the shadows, heading for Bella Tait's house. In the light of a street lamp, Christine glanced down at the flick knife in her hand. She flicked it open as she approached Donald Tait's car. She paused and stared at the Tait's house with its dark rooms behind drawn curtains. Nothing and nobody stirred in the street. Not even PC Stan Cooper was awake at that time of the morning.

Kev, her latest boyfriend, was an expert car thief and had taught her a lot. She knew how to break into a car and how to jump-start it but that wasn't why she was standing beside Donald Tait's car that night.

"What if I want the driver to have an accident?" Christine had asked Kev. "What could I do to make that happen?"

Kev had stared at her.

"Why would you want to do that?"

"Just interested, is all. So 'ow'd you do it?"

"Best way is to do the brakes. You have to get under the car."

Kev had pointed to one of the hydraulic tubes.

"See that rubber tube?" he had said, as they lay beneath his car, and Christine had nodded.

"Well, if you cut it, the driver ain't got no brakes after a while."

"After a while? What yer mean, after a while?"

Kev had shrugged but Christine seemed satisfied. She smiled to herself, a plan developing in her mind. That plan was the reason why she now found herself standing next to Bella's father's car.

Christine smiled. Now, with Kev's directions clear in her mind, she checked the windows in the street for one last time. Curtains tightly drawn. All clear.

Although the car was parked under a street light, nobody saw her slide on her back underneath, and, using her lighter to see, deftly slice the brake line with her blade.

Her work was done. Silently, she left the scene and disappeared into the inky darkness.

Next morning dawned bright. As the birds in the hedgerows greeted the day, Jayne Fairweather was putting the key in the lock of the Post Office. A family of ducks crossed the road, intent on reaching the pond on the village green.

"It all happened in slow motion," Jayne said later to PC Cooper, who was taking notes. "Don Tait was driving down the road as he always does that time in the morning. I was raising my arm to wave to him when I saw the ducks crossing the road. Don must have seen them at exactly the same time, but instead of slowing down and stopping, he swerved to miss them and drove straight into the village pond! I tell you, I couldn't believe my eyes!"

Stan Cooper was tempted to chuckle but restrained himself. Donald Tait hadn't been injured and neither had the ducks. No harm done. Except Mr Tait claimed that his brake cable had been severed. Now that wasn't the sort of thing that happened in Sixpenny Cross, and it wasn't funny.

It hadn't taken long for Archie Draper to arrive in his tractor and pull the car out of the pond. Strangely, Bella

Tait's missing bicycle was found at the same time.

In Yewbridge, Christine listened to the local news on the radio. Nothing. No mention of deaths or cars spinning out of control. Her eyes narrowed into slits and she was filled with rage.

bbbbb

In 1973, Pink Floyd released *Dark Side of the Moon* and Princess Anne announced her engagement to Captain Mark Phillips.

Bella Tait had the world at her feet.

She read the letter from Bristol University for the umpteenth time.

...*We are therefore pleased to offer you a place studying Veterinary Sciences*...

"I can't believe it," said June, shaking her head. "Our little Bella going off to university to train to be a vet!"

"*La mia bella* Bella, we're so proud of you!"

"Thanks, Dad!"

"We're going to miss you, Bella," her mother said. "Make some space on the table, I've made a plate of hazelnut *biscotti* to celebrate."

"I wonder how Red is doing?" Bella wondered, nibbling on *biscotti*.

"Oh, he'll be starting university somewhere as well, I expect," said June. "Such a bright boy, he'll do well."

They'd promised each other to keep in touch, but the long-distance relationship was hard to sustain and they exchanged letters less and less often. One day, Bella's letter to Red was returned, unopened, marked *unknown at this address*. She didn't write again.

They say good luck breeds more good luck, and that may be true because, apart from Bella being offered a university place, another piece of welcome news arrived within the week.

"We've done it! We've finally done it!" yelled Donald.

He had the Yewbridge Gazette spread open before him on the dining room table, and was comparing it with his Littlewoods Pools coupon.

"Done what?" asked June, coming in, flour on her hands.

"We've won the pools!" said Donald. "Well, not the big prize, but if I've done my sums right, there'll be enough money to get Bella all set up at university. And there'll be enough to do repairs on the house. We can fix those loose tiles on the roof, for instance. Best of all, there'll still be enough for us to book a holiday to Italy! We're going to see your grandmother's village at last!"

June sat down heavily, her floury hands clutching her heart.

"Oh, Donald, are we? Are you sure? Are we really?"

"Yes! We're really going to Italy!"

"What's this?" asked Bella coming into the room. "What's happened?"

"We've won some money on the football pools! Enough to give us a holiday in Italy and set you up for university!"

Bella gaped at him.

"That's fantastic," she said at last. "Really good, but I don't think I'll come with you to Italy, if you don't mind."

"Oh Bella, why ever not? We can afford it," said June.

"It's not that, it's just that I only have a few short weeks before uni starts, and they've sent me a long reading list. I'd like to do some studying in advance, and I need time to get packed up, too. You go without me this time, I'm sure there'll be other chances."

"You're right *la mia bella* Bella, your future is more important at the moment. There will always be another time. But we won't go until you are settled at university."

The next weeks were filled with packing and anticipation. The whole family went to Yewbridge and bought suitcases.

"Going away, are you?" asked the girl at the sales counter.

"My husband and I are going to Italy to see the village my grandmother was born in," said June, her eyes dancing.

"Oh, that'll be nice," said the assistant. "Room for me in that suitcase, by any chance? Brrr, I can feel winter arriving here already. Bet it's lovely and the sun is shining in Italy."

June beamed, already feeling the Italian sun on her skin in her imagination.

For Bella, they bought bedding, clothes, stationery, a kettle, mugs and various other bits and pieces. Never had the Taits splashed out on so many items on one single occasion. It was a happy day, finished off by Donald treating them all to a meal at an Italian restaurant.

"To get us in the mood," he said.

"Just think!" said June excitedly. "Next month we'll be eating real Italian food in Italy!"

"Let's raise our glasses to Bella's future and our Italian holiday!" said Donald.

As the ruby chianti sparkled in the candlelight, all three members of the Tait family clinked glasses and sipped.

Bella had ordered all her text books, and when they arrived, she began studying like never before. She was determined to shine at university.

June was permanently pink with excitement and could talk about nothing but the coming trip to Italy.

"We've booked one of those newfangled package holidays," she told Jayne Fairweather. "When we arrive, the holiday company will take us to our hotel. On the first morning there's a welcome meeting and we can book excursions if we want. I want to see *everything*. Donald says we should hire a car for a few days too, then we can visit my grandmother's village."

"Sounds heavenly," said Jayne, dusting off a row of canned beans. "I could do with a holiday myself."

"Thank you so much for looking after Bella's pets while we're away," said June. "That is really kind of you."

"Just you concentrate on having a good holiday," said Jayne. "You deserve it."

bbbb

"Bye, darling," said June, hugging her daughter. "We'll see you in a few weeks."

Taking leave of her daughter at university was just as hard as that day, years ago, when she had left Bella in the classroom on her first day of school. She looked around the student room, with its two beds, two wardrobes and two desks. It seemed stark and unhomely.

"I'll be fine, honestly," said Bella, reading her mother's mind. "Once I've unpacked and put my own bits and pieces around, it'll be just like home. Don't worry about me, I want you to have a wonderful holiday. I can't wait to hear all about it, so make sure you send me some postcards!"

"*Ciao, la mia bella* Bella," said her father and enveloped her in his arms. "Enjoy yourself, don't work too hard, and remember, we're so proud of you!"

When they'd gone, the first item Bella unpacked was the wooden box that Red had made for her.

"That's pretty," said Susan, Bella's roommate. "Are those your initials?"

"Yes, a friend made it for me."

Bella finished putting her books in the bookcase, filled

her new kettle with water and plugged it into the socket.

"Would you like a cup of tea?"

"Yes, please," said Susan, serious eyes regarding Bella. "It all feels so strange, doesn't it? Have you ever been away from home before?"

"No," said Bella, popping a tea bag into each cup.

Had she been at home, her mother would never have used tea bags. She'd have used a teapot, with proper tea leaves, and she'd have left it for a few minutes to 'brew'. A pang of homesickness clutched at Bella's heart.

"Me neither," said Susan. "Everybody seems nice though. And we can always go home at weekends."

"My parents are going on holiday to Italy, so I'll wait until they come back."

"Oh, lucky them!"

"Do you take sugar in your tea?"

"No, thank you."

Bella passed the mug to Susan, then ladled three heaped spoons into her own and stirred until a whirlpool formed in the centre.

She watched the whirlpool slow, then cease altogether.

I mustn't keep thinking about Mum and Dad, and the animals, and Sixpenny Cross, she thought. *I want to be a vet. That's all that matters.*

It was excellent advice, but then Bella didn't know what would happen next.

Chapter Ten

"Bella, I've brought the post. Looks like you've got a postcard from Italy!" said Susan, handing over a few letters to her roommate.

"Thanks!"

Bella ignored the other letters and stared at the picture on the postcard. The scene was of a donkey with panniers strapped to its back. An old man was leading it through a sun-drenched vineyard.

She turned it over, and read the words in her mother's familiar handwriting.

> *Darling Bella, Italy is just heavenly as I knew it would be. Hotel is nice, food lovely and weather very warm. Missing you of course. Hiring car tomorrow. Daddy sends love and lots of xxx*

Bella smiled. She could picture her mother in her new sunhat, basking in the Italian sunshine, revelling in the fact that she was finally visiting the country where her ancestors had lived.

"Looks like they are having a fantastic time," she said to Susan.

She stared at the picture for a long time, reading the words over and over again before finally slipping the postcard into her polished wooden box along with her other treasures.

University life and the many lectures and activities kept Bella very busy. The overwhelming homesickness she suffered in the first days retreated. She and Susan became good friends, the first friendship Bella had forged since Red left.

A few days later, while Bella was working at her desk, Susan came in with more mail.

"Looks like another postcard from Italy," she said, dropping the card on Bella's desk.

This time it was written in her father's scrawly hand, the characters small in order to fit more words in the space provided.

La mia bella Bella, having a wonderful time. We found the village and it's just how we imagined. Made friends with a fisherman who knew your grandmother's family. He's taking us on his boat tomorrow! Miss you, but will see you soon and tell all! Don't work too hard.
Love you, Dad xxx

The picture showed white frothy waves lapping at a sandy beach. On the horizon, tiny sailing boats dotted the turquoise ocean.

Bella popped the postcard into her box and hugged herself. She'd be seeing them this weekend!

The plan was that on Saturday she would catch an early train to Yewbridge. Her father would pick her up from the railway station and take her home to Sixpenny Cross.

Her mother would have coffee and cakes waiting on the table and she imagined the feel of her father's arms around her. She couldn't wait to hear all about their holiday and to tell them about her course and university life.

In Sixpenny Cross, Jayne Fairweather turned the key in the lock and opened the Taits' front door. Her daily visit to water the plants and feed the animals had taught Hattie to listen for the key in the door, knowing she was about to be fed.

"Hello, Hattie," said Jayne, bending down to smooth the purring cat. "Pleased to see me, are you?"

Jayne hummed as she did her usual rounds. First she went into the kitchen and fed Hattie. The little cat wound around her ankles until she set the bowl down. Jayne washed her hands at the sink, running her eye along June's shelf of cookbooks. *Pasta like Mama Makes, 100 Italian Recipes, Italian Farmhouse Kitchen.* The titles made her feel quite hungry.

Next she fed the hamsters, the guinea pigs and put birdseed in the budgie's cage.

I'll give the plants one last drop of water, she thought. *June and Donald will be back tomorrow.*

As the water splashed into the watering can, the doorbell rang.

Whoever could that be?

Jayne turned off the tap and went to open the door.

PC Stan Cooper stood before her, his policeman's helmet held in both hands. A lady wearing navy blue uniform and a jaunty hat stood beside him.

"Stan!" exclaimed Jayne. "Don and June are away in Italy until tomorrow."

"I know," said Stan. His knuckles were white. "I wasn't sure if Miss Tait was here or not. I'm accompanying Miss Travis."

The lady took this as her cue and stepped forward.

"Forgive me," she said, "am I correct in saying that this is the Taits' house?"

"Yes, that's right," said Jayne, and Stan nodded. "I'm afraid they are away at the moment, can I help?"

"I'm representing Mr and Mrs Tait's travel company. May I ask who you are?"

"I'm Jayne Fairweather, I own Sixpenny Cross shop and Post Office. I'm a family friend, just feeding the animals and watering the plants."

"May we come in?" Miss Travis asked.

Dumbly, Jayne opened the door wider, and let Stan and the lady in, then showed them to the sitting room. Miss Travis sat down, but Stan remained standing, rocking on his heels, still clutching his policeman's helmet before him.

"PC Cooper tells me that Mr and Mrs Tait's next of kin is their daughter, Bella?" the lady began. She was sitting very upright, her briefcase on her knees.

"Yes. She's at Bristol University. She's studying to be a vet."

"I will need to see her in person. Do you know where she is exactly?"

"Yes, I have her student hall address. Listen, what's this all about? Can you not just tell me?"

The woman paused, unsure what to say next.

"I'm afraid it's against company rules."

"Oh for goodness' sake! Has something happened to June and Donald?"

The woman stared at Jayne for a moment, then glanced up at Stan. He nodded, giving her permission to continue.

"I'm sorry to have to tell you that Mr and Mrs Tait were reported drowned yesterday. We believe they were in a fishing boat when a sudden squall arose and the boat capsized. Nobody survived and the boat and bodies have been recovered."

Jayne's heart pounded and her mouth went dry.

"No. There must be some mistake."

"I'm so sorry."

"They were due home tomorrow."

"Yes."

Jayne stared at the stranger opposite her, then at Stan. His eyes were downcast. June's clock ticked on the mantlepiece.

"Are you sure it was them?" she said at last. "There must be lots of tourists…" Her voice trailed away.

"I'm so sorry. The fisherman was identified and hotel staff verified that the bodies were those of June and Donald Tait."

Jayne sat still, trying to absorb the information and accept the fact that she'd never see her friends again.

"What about Bella?"

"If you could give me Bella's contact details, I'll drive over to Bristol immediately and inform her."

"No! Bella adores her parents, she can't hear this from a stranger!"

"Perhaps you could accompany me?"

This was a nightmare. A complete nightmare.

Jayne closed her eyes, breathed deeply and nodded.

Bella. How was the poor girl going to take the news?

"We should go now," she said. "This is not something that we can delay."

Chapter Eleven

Jayne Fairweather read the label. *Room 64, Susan Brown, Bella Tait.* She tapped on the door.

"Come in!" called Susan.

Jayne opened the door and stepped inside, her uniformed companion close behind. Bella looked up and could hardly believe her eyes.

"Auntie Jayne! Wow! What a lovely surprise!"

She leaped up and flew across the room to give her a hug. Susan smiled and wondered who the accompanying lady in uniform was.

"Bella…"

"Did you come especially to see me? How lovely! How's Hattie? Has she been missing Mum and Dad? And the hamsters? And the guinea pigs?"

"Bella…"

"Did you get a postcard from Italy? Look, I got two."

Bella's wooden box was open on the desk and she reached for the postcards to show Jayne. Jayne stopped her hand.

"Bella," she said, pulling her down to sit beside her on the bed, not letting go of her hand.

Susan and the lady in uniform watched. Something icy gripped Susan's heart. This was not a normal visit.

"What's the matter?" asked Bella, suddenly aware that the atmosphere was all wrong. She looked deep into Jayne's eyes and all colour drained from her face. A glance at the uniformed lady confirmed her fears.

"It's something to do with Mum and Dad, isn't it? Something terrible has happened!"

Jayne tried, but her throat had closed up and she couldn't speak. Huge tears filled her eyes and ran unchecked down her cheeks.

Miss Travis stepped forward.

"I'm so sorry," she said, "I'm afraid we have very bad news."

bbbbb

The university was sympathetic and helpful. Bella's tutors agreed to extend their deadlines and save lecture notes for her return.

They needn't have bothered. Bella's passion for her studies died the day she was told that her parents had drowned.

"Bella, you should think about going back to university," said Jayne, two months after the tragic event.

Bella shook her head.

"I'm not ready," she said, burying her face in Hattie's soft fur.

Hattie was an elderly cat now. No longer was she a threat to birds, and her days were spent sleeping in sun puddles, only moving when the sun swung round.

Jayne sighed. The last weeks had been tough. The bodies had been flown back, and their funeral was attended by the whole shocked village. Bella's parents had been buried side by side in the churchyard, a single gravestone marking their final resting place. Across its dark surface, chiselled in letters of gold, the inscription read:

My wonderful, beloved parents,
June and Donald Tait.

*You were tragically lost at sea
but never from my heart.
Your adoring daughter, Bella.*

Thankfully, Donald had taken out travel insurance and the payout covered all expenses. Her parents had also insured their lives so Bella would never need to find money to pay the mortgage on the house. There was a sizable lump sum too, and if Bella was careful, it would keep her for a long time. At least until she finished training and started her career.

But Bella could scarcely get up in the morning, let alone plan her career. The only reason she rose at all was to care for the animals, and she only dressed when she needed to go out for supplies.

Jayne was desperately worried. Bella refused to open the curtains which had been drawn since her parents died. She wouldn't touch June and Donald's bedroom, or clear anything in the cottage. Her mother's cookbooks were set out exactly as she had left them. The novel she was halfway through lay open on her bedside table. Her father's spare spectacles were still on the coffee table. The house was a shrine to their memory.

"Let me help you sort through their things," Jayne suggested gently.

"No, I'm not ready."

Bella's eyes were dull and lifeless, and her voice had taken on a monotonous quality. The house was growing more and more disordered and Bella made no attempt to tidy or clean it.

Bella's lost interest in everything, Jayne thought as she walked home. *And I don't know what I can do to help her.*

Jayne lived alone a few doors down from Bella, just a short walk away. She was so deep in thought, she almost didn't notice the heap on her doorstep.

A shivering, dirty, brown and white dog looked up at her from under heavy lids.

"Good gracious, where did *you* come from?" she said.

The dog wagged its tail weakly, but didn't seem capable of more.

Jayne opened her front door and let herself in. The dog questioned her with sad eyes, then got to its feet and followed her in, before collapsing again in the hall.

"You wait there," said Jayne. "I'll see what I can find for you."

The dog looked too exhausted to move, so Jayne filled a bowl with water, and another with the leftover chicken she was planning to eat for her supper that night.

"Here you are, Sad Eyes," she said. "Let's see if this makes you feel any better."

As the dog ate and drank, Jayne thought about her new problem. She couldn't keep a dog. She worked at the Post Office every day and the shop sold food. Animals, apart from guide dogs, were not allowed in food stores. No, the dog would have to find another home.

It suddenly dawned on her that she knew exactly who might want this mangy heap of fur. Bella! With luck, the dog might bring a sparkle back to the girl's eyes.

She dialled Bella's number.

Bella was standing in the kitchen. She should eat, but her appetite had left her the moment she heard of her parents' tragic death.

She'd recently caught sight of herself in the bathroom mirror and had been surprised.

Is that really me? she asked her reflection.

The weight was dropping off, which wasn't a bad thing,

but where did those dark rings round her eyes come from? And had her hair always been so lank and dull? Surely it used to shine with health?

On the counter in front of her was her polished box. She ran her fingertips over its smooth surface then over the wonderful, elaborate engraving of her initials. She opened the box, gazing at her treasures.

There was the old photograph of her Italian great-grandmother, dressed in black, leaning on a walking stick. The elderly lady looked sad.

I wonder if she approved of her daughter marrying an Englishman, she thought. *I wish I'd known her.*

She picked up her mother's wedding ring and stroked her cheek with it. The gold felt warm, as though it been recently worn. Then she picked up the precious postcards.

La mia bella Bella...

She could almost hear her father's gentle voice. She imagined him choosing this particular postcard, knowing they were going out on a boat trip.

Tears streamed down her cheeks, blurring the image of the little boats bobbing on the Ionian sea.

Why did you have to go out in that fishing boat that day? Why, why, why?

The phone rang.

Bella considered ignoring it, but she wiped her tears away on her sleeve, walked into the living room and reluctantly picked up the receiver.

Chapter Twelve

"Hello Bella, it's me again."

"Auntie Jayne? Did you forget something?"

So Jayne told Bella all about Sad Eyes.

"Of course, I can't keep a dog," she said. "So I wondered whether you may like to look after it? Perhaps when it's cleaned up a bit, and given a few good meals, we could find someone to adopt it."

"Of course! Do you want to bring the dog round now?"

For the first time in weeks, Jayne sensed a little animation in Bella's voice.

"No, I'll pop round in the morning. It's had a good feed and it looks exhausted, so I'm going to shut it in the hall for the night."

Bella suddenly had a purpose. When she went to bed that night, she was actually looking forward to the next day. And that hadn't happened for weeks.

The next morning, before heading to the Post Office, Jayne led Sad Eyes to Bella's house using a makeshift leash and collar.

"She's a little more perky today," she said to Bella. "And I discovered she's already been trained to walk with a leash. Poor thing must be lost."

Bella crouched down to examine the dog.

"I can see why you call her Sad Eyes," she said. "And you're quite right, it's a girl. She's so hairy I can't see if she has an injury. I don't think she has fleas though. I'll keep her under observation for twenty-four hours and let her settle in, then I'll examine her properly tomorrow."

"Good. I'll pop some dog food round from the shop later. And I'll put up a card in the Post Office in case anybody has lost a dog, though I don't remember ever seeing this one in Sixpenny Cross."

Not only did Sad Eyes know how to walk on a leash, she also knew all about cats. When Hattie walked into the room and saw Sad Eyes, she froze, her fur standing on end, her tail twice its usual size. Sad Eyes wagged her tail briefly, then ignored her. Hattie, although still wide-eyed, decided that the newcomer was not a threat. She jumped up to the windowsill, chose a spot, then walked round in circles before curling up for a nap in the sun.

"You really are a very nice, polite dog," said Bella. "And I shan't call you Sad Eyes, although it fits. I shall call you Sadie."

Sadie twitched her tail in acknowledgement.

Bella watched Sadie carefully all day. Sadie ate hungrily and drank water, but she seemed to lack energy.

That night Bella made her a comfortable bed in the kitchen, but Sadie wouldn't settle. She preferred to lie under the stairs, so Bella moved the bedding to Sadie's chosen spot.

"Good night," she said. "Tomorrow I'll examine you properly and maybe even give you a bath."

She climbed the stairs to her bedroom, averting her eyes as she passed her parents' room. Hattie was already fast asleep on her bed.

Bella slept, and for the first time in weeks she was not tortured by terrifying nightmares of tiny boats battered by wild waves, or cries for help drowned by the wind.

The next morning, she scampered downstairs to see how Sadie was doing in the cupboard under the stairs. Hattie followed at a more dignified pace.

"Sadie?"

Sadie didn't get up to greet her, but briefly thumped her tail. Bella sensed something was different. She snapped on the light then gaped at the dog at her feet.

Sadie was lying on her side. Firmly attached to her were seven tiny, squirming, newborn puppies.

"Oh my!" breathed Bella, crouching down.

Sadie's wet nose nudged her hand. She looked at Bella and twitched her tail a few times, as if to say, *hey, I did a good job, didn't I?*

fffff

The card Jayne Fairweather pinned up in the Post Office attracted no response except curiosity.

Found

Medium-sized brown and white, long-haired mongrel dog. Friendly and well-trained.

Please apply within.

"Oh," said PC Stan Cooper, "I see a dog has been found? Who's looking after it?"

"Bella Tait," said Jayne. "Actually, I was just going to take down that card and rewrite it a little. Bella phoned me a few minutes ago and it seems that the poor dog was not only homeless, but pregnant. She just gave birth to seven puppies under Bella's stairs."

"Oh my goodness," said Stan as he tried to pull on his leather policemen's gloves.

It was December, and the wind was cold. Wearing gloves when riding a bike in such cold was a necessity. A few minutes earlier his gloves had fitted him perfectly but now they were proving to be a struggle to pull on.

"I think you've got your gloves on the wrong hands," observed Jayne.

Stan Cooper's clumsiness was legendary amongst the residents of Sixpenny Cross. Like his father before him, he was an excellent policeman and well suited to the village where crime was rare and an understanding of the locals essential. He was liked by all, and his clumsiness was regarded with affection and accepted.

"Thanks," said Stan, switching the gloves over and successfully pulling them on. "Please wish Miss Tait well with those pups. I may even take one off her hands later if she's looking to find homes for them."

He put his policeman's helmet back on, and left the shop.

Jayne rewrote the card.

Found

Very pregnant, medium-sized brown and white, long-haired mongrel dog. Friendly and well-trained.

Please apply within.

The cell doors clanged shut. The prison warder's rubber-soled shoes squeaked as she walked along the corridor. The lights would be dimmed soon and the inmates were expected to sleep. Judging by the shouting and banging on the bars, few of the women were tired.

Christine Dayton wasn't happy, but then she seldom was. The Young Offenders' Institution they put her in first had been awful, but it had been a walk in the park compared with Her Majesty's Women's Prison, Holloway.

"You will be detained until you have learned that theft is not acceptable in our society," the magistrate had declared.

Sitting on the bed in her shared cell, she gnawed on her nails, trying to shut out the shouting of the inmates as they communicated with each other.

London had seemed so attractive compared with Yewbridge. Of course she knew the streets wouldn't be paved with gold but she thought finding a job and making a living would be easy in such a large city. Unfortunately, her poor attitude and lack of respect for those in authority ensured that she never kept a job for more than a few days.

Sleeping under the arches with the other homeless people and runaways wasn't so bad. She'd always been able to look after herself.

And learning how to break into people's houses and help herself to their possessions wasn't difficult either. She'd had plenty of practice in Sixpenny Cross. It was easy if you were careful.

She'd become an expert burglar and accomplished shoplifter. Then, when she'd been caught and sent to the Young Offenders' Institution, she'd mixed with others just like herself and honed her skills.

She learned how to jostle someone to distract them, whilst relieving them of their wallet.

She learned how to target householders and memorise their routines. She'd watch for the best time to break in, like when a mother was collecting kids from school.

She learned how to spy and take note where people hid their house keys. Amazing how many idiots hid keys under a flowerpot or doormat. Or left their doors open.

She learned how to find the blind spots in a store, where the security cameras didn't reach. And how to try on clothes in a changing room, and put one's own clothes back on top. Then walk out, bold as brass.

But her luck had run out, and now here she was in Holloway for a stretch. Caught again. And it was a lot worse than the Young Offenders' Unit.

I wonder what that spoilt Fat Belly Bella is doin' now? That's if she ain't exploded. I bet she's at some stupid university, and that quarter-Italian mother of 'ers is still fillin' her up with pasta. And I bet 'er dad phones 'er every day. Loser!

When I get out of here, I might just leave London and take myself back to Yewbridge and the countryside. Lots of villages. All ripe for the picking. Might even pay smug lil Fat Belly and her parents a visit.

When they've gone out.

Chapter Thirteen

Bella was distracted for the first time since she'd lost her parents. Helping animals was what she lived for and what she did best, allowing little time for brooding.

Sadie was an excellent mother. She washed and fed her babies continually, and watched that they didn't stray too far. Bella loved looking after Sadie, and she loved watching the puppies grow.

"Those pups are going to open their eyes soon. And it won't be two minutes before they'll be under our feet and all over the place," observed Jayne on one of her regular visits. "Shall I help you have a bit of a tidy up? This pile of newspapers, and this empty box, for instance. Shall I take them outside and pop them in the bin?"

"No," said Bella. "No, thank you. Those newspapers could be useful for the pups when I'm house-training them. And I have plans for that box."

"Well, what about these empty cans?"

"No."

"Bella, you have to throw *some* things away. It's getting pretty cluttered in here. What about this empty bottle?"

"No, I'm going to use that."

Jayne gave up.

Apart from the untidy house, Jayne was pleased with Bella's progress. Sadie's arrival had given Bella a purpose, and Jayne hoped that when the pups and Sadie left for new homes, Bella might return to university and pick up her studies.

But Jayne would be disappointed because it didn't work out at all like that.

Christmas came and went, and the weeks slipped by. It was 1974 and Britain was in the grip of the coal miners' strike. The numerous power stations that depended on coal to generate electricity were forced to shut down and a three-day week was introduced in an effort to conserve energy. A general election was called, resulting in Edward Heath's resignation and Harold Wilson becoming Prime Minister.

By March, Sadie's pups were ready for new homes. Jayne was concerned that Bella had made no attempt to have the puppies adopted, and the cottage was filled with the yaps of seven young dogs and beginning to look the worse for wear.

"Bella, shall I put a postcard up in the Post Office and see if we can't get these pups adopted?" she asked. "Hey, stop that!"

This remark was directed to a pup whose sharp little teeth were sunk into the hem of her skirt, playing tug of war.

"There's no hurry," said Bella. "They're doing well here."

"Are those puppies of Miss Tait's ready for adoption yet?" asked PC Cooper a day later, popping his head round the Post Office door.

"Well, yes, and no," replied Jayne. "They are old enough now, but whether you can persuade Bella to part with them is another matter."

"I'll have a go," he said, grinning. "I'll pay her a visit."

He walked up Bella Tait's path and tapped on the peeling front door. Her father had been planning to sand down the door and revarnish it in spring.

His knock set off a chorus of yaps from within.

"Hold on, I'll just shut the puppies away," Bella called, then opened the door, her face blanching when she saw PC Cooper on her doorstep.

"It's okay, Miss Tait," said Stan hurriedly. "I'm not here on police business. I heard you had some puppies and wondered whether I might see them."

"Of course!" said Bella, suddenly more cheerful. "Please come in."

Stan stepped inside, and his shiny leather boot landed in a pile of puppy poo that should have been cleared up.

Bella opened the door to the kitchen and seven fat, hairy, brown and white pups tumbled out. In the lead was one with a patch over one eye and hair that stuck up at all angles.

Stan crouched down and the puppy stopped tugging at his shoelaces long enough to smother the policeman's face with wet licks.

"Hey, Tufty, good to meet you!" said Stan, picking up the wriggling, affectionate puppy.

"I think you've made a friend there!" said Bella.

"Are they ready to leave their mother yet?"

"No," Bella said quickly, almost snatching the puppy from his arms, "not nearly ready yet."

"I'd love to adopt young Tufty here, would that be okay? He'd live at the police house with me, not far away at all. Perhaps I could call back for him in a couple of weeks?"

"Well, I don't know… I'll contact you when I feel they are ready to go."

Stan had to be satisfied with that.

✥✥✥✥✥

Weeks turned into months and the puppies grew. Bella turned away PC Cooper and all prospective owners. Jayne

Fairweather worried more and more about the state of Bella's home and her health. It was only a small house, and the puppies and other animals filled it.

Word had trickled round the village that Bella rescued animals. Jayne Fairweather was partly responsible for this because, in an effort to help Bella, she'd put up a postcard in the Post Office saying:

Wanted

Old towels, blankets or quilts to be used for animal rescue. Please drop them here or at Bella Tait's house. Thank you!

People brought their old blankets and quilts, but they also brought all manner of animals and wildlife for Bella to nurse and care for. The house began to fill up with rescued and injured animals and Bella needed to make space to accommodate them all.

The living room was mainly given over to Sadie and her puppies. The pups had grown big and their boisterous behaviour was ruining the furniture and carpet. Sharp puppy teeth had shredded the curtains and chewed the upholstery. A window was broken, and roughly boarded up. Bella dragged one big chair into the front garden, uncertain what to do with it next. And in spite of her efforts, the room smelled of urine and puppy poo. Hattie sought peace on the mantlepiece.

Her mother's dining room was now unrecognisable. Chair legs were chewed, crates sat on top of each other, some with occupants, others empty but not cleaned out. Those that were occupied contained a pigeon with a broken wing, other injured birds, and even a barn owl that had flown into a power line. There were rabbits, both wild and domesticated, white rats that bred alarmingly, and guinea pigs, either abandoned or injured. There were hedgehogs, a ferret and mice.

The crates spilled over into the kitchen leaving just enough space for Bella to prepare the animals' food. A small area was set aside for a pair of scales to weigh her patients and keep notes on their progress.

Henrietta, the chicken, marched in and out of the house as she pleased. In the front garden, her mother's carefully tended flowers were neglected and the weeds allowed to take over. The easy chair from the living room sat rotting. The once neat picket fence had slats missing and leaned drunkenly.

Bella shared her bedroom with an assortment of rescued cats and two litters of kittens. Apart from her late parents' bedroom, which remained untouched with the door firmly closed, the house was full to bursting.

There wasn't a label for the condition in those days, but Bella had become an animal hoarder. Her whole life was taken up by caring for the animals.

Bella threw herself into the job of nursing her patients and tending the orphaned and abandoned creatures.

At least I have no time to think about Mum and Dad, she thought as she ladled dog food into bowls. *These animals depend on me.*

Mr Dodd, the bank manager, was not so sympathetic. His expression was severe as he stared at Bella over the top of his horn-rimmed spectacles.

"Miss Tait, you must curb your spending. If you carry on at this rate, you'll use up all your inheritance in no time."

Bella stared back at him.

"But I have to feed the animals," she said.

Mr Dodd blinked.

"Miss Tait, there'll be no money to feed *yourself* if you

don't cut back."

✂✂✂✂

"Sign here," said the prison warder.

Christine scrawled her name on the dotted line.

The warder handed her a plastic bag containing an opened packet of cigarettes, a lighter and some small change, Christine's belongings before she had been admitted to Holloway.

"You know that you must report to your probation officer? If you don't, you'll be straight back in here."

"Yes, I know."

As if I'm gonna bother with that!

"Right," said the warder wearily, "here's your allowance, a gift from Her Majesty the Queen. And here's your probation officer's phone number, and the address of the halfway house. They're expecting you." She unlocked the metal door and pushed it open. A blast of cold air swirled in. "Off you go then, good luck."

Christine stepped out into the street and sucked the grey London air into her lungs. The prison gate clanged shut behind her. There was nobody to meet her but she didn't care.

Freedom! At last!

With a spring in her step she walked down the street, heading for the bus stop. The money in her pocket wasn't going to last long so she'd better top it up. And where was a sure-fire place to acquire some? On the platforms of the good old London underground, of course.

A bus approached just as she reached the bus stop.

"Where you goin', Miss?" asked the conductor.

"Caledonian Road, please," she said.

Yes, just one underground stop away from King's Cross, on the Piccadilly line. A nice busy platform. Perfect!

Chapter Fourteen

Bella sat hunched on the doorstep of her cottage with her head buried in her hands. Behind the closed front door she could hear thumps and yaps from inside. The puppies, adorable as they were, had become adolescent wreckers. The inside of the cottage was ruined, even Bella acknowledged that. Her mother would turn in her grave if she could see how her cottage looked now.

Tears trickled from Bella's eyes. She was so tired. Worrying kept her awake most of the night and even when she slept, nightmares tormented her.

How had it got so bad?

The event that Mr Dodd, the bank manager, had predicted, was nearly upon her. She had almost run out of money.

Who will look after the animals if I can't? They'll starve!

Fresh tears sprang from her eyes. She shuddered and sobbed into her hands, shoulders heaving.

"Bella?"

Bella was too wrapped in her own misery to hear the voice or see the figure in front of her.

"Bella? Is that you? Whatever is the matter?"

Bella paused. Choking back a sob, she tilted her head slightly and peeped through her fingers. Who was this tall, slim man with a thatch of deep auburn hair? He was a stranger, yet he looked familiar. She gasped, and her hands fell away from her pale, tear-streaked face.

"Red?"

Red smiled into her bloodshot eyes.

"Yup! It's me all right! I think I came back just in time, didn't I?" He plonked himself down on the doorstep beside her and draped his arm around her shoulders. "I'm here to help."

Bella gaped at him.

"Now, before you tell me what the tears are all about, explain to me what's causing the thumping and barking behind us in the house. Has a circus moved in?"

"It's the puppies," wailed Bella and, burying her face into his chest, renewed her sobbing.

Red held her and stared over her head, waiting for her to quieten. He didn't show it, but he was shocked to see the tumbledown fence and the unkempt front garden. But only when Bella's sobs turned to hiccups did he speak.

"Bella, before you tell me everything, I want to tell you some stuff you need to know."

Bella was silent, listening. Only an occasional hiccup escaped her.

"When my family moved to Scotland all those years ago, I was miserable. I'd lost my best friend and nobody could take your place, Bella. I used to watch the postman like a hawk, in case he brought me a letter from you. Then one day, it struck me. If you felt the same as I did, you would be miserable, too. So I forced myself to write less and less often. I was trying to help you to move on, you understand? Then, one black day I wrote *unknown at this address* on your envelope and posted it back to you."

Bella stared at him.

"I never wrote again after that," she whispered.

"I know," he sighed. "I thought I'd done it for the best."

"Did you go to university?" asked Bella.

"No. My parents wanted me to, but I fought it. I'm afraid I became a rebellious teenager and got myself into a lot of trouble. I started drinking."

Bella drew away from him in order to stare into his face.

"Are you serious?"

"Yes, absolutely serious. I found it was a good way to hide from life. I started drinking because I wanted to escape, and now I drink because I need to."

"You... You're an alcoholic?"

"I believe I am. Then, a couple of days ago, I was sitting drinking, and I thought of you. And I felt as though you were in trouble. The impression just wouldn't leave me. I tried drowning the feeling but the whiskey tasted horrible on my tongue. Eventually, I lost patience. I decided I had to travel down and see you for myself, put my mind at rest."

"Two days ago?"

Bella recalled the fitful night she'd had two nights ago, robbed of sleep by worry. *Help me!* she'd sobbed into her pillow, not knowing who she was calling upon.

"Yes. I stopped fighting the feeling and packed up my worldly goods. They are in that holdall over there by the gate. I told my landlord that I wouldn't be coming back, and I caught a train to London, then another to Yewbridge. Then I walked from Yewbridge to Sixpenny Cross. And here I am, at your service, ma'am."

Bella stared at him anew, still shocked to the core.

"It's your turn," he said gently. "I've told you all my secrets."

Bella swallowed. She had no idea where to start.

"How are your parents?" asked Red, trying to be helpful.

Bella's face crumpled.

"They're dead!" she whispered, "They drowned in Italy."

bbbbb

Christine was in her element, the adrenalin rushing. It was five o'clock on the Piccadilly line, and the underground platform was crowded.

Lights flashed and the dull, distant rumble of an approaching train grew in volume. The train slid to a halt by the platform and its doors whooshed open. The crowds surged forward, jostling and pushing, and Christine was in the thick of it.

Nobody noticed Christine's skinny arm snake out and dip first into a commuter's pocket, then into a shopper's bag. In a split second, light fingers found what they sought: a wallet and a purse.

The doors closed and the train rolled away leaving nobody on the platform but Christine and new passengers just arriving.

Christine locked herself into a public toilet and stripped the wallet and purse of cash.

Lovely! Enough money for a nice meal, a bottle of wine and a decent room in a hotel.

She threw away the plundered wallet and purse and stuffed pound notes into her pocket.

Too easy!

She was enjoying herself. She'd get some more money together, then, when she felt like it, she'd head south to Sixpenny Cross and look up a few old 'friends'.

Christine hummed to herself as she tipped the lavatory attendant and returned to the platform to target more victims.

bbbbb

The sun dipped behind Sixpenny Woods and bats flitted round the street lamps snatching dizzy moths. Bella and

Red were oblivious to the world as they talked.

"And now I have all these animals to look after…"

"What animals?"

"Well, there's Hattie of course. And the mice and guinea pigs. But…I…I seem to have set up a kind of animal rescue centre."

Red stared at her, waiting.

"I have dogs, a whole litter of puppies! Stray cats and their kittens, wildlife like hedgehogs and birds… I even have a chicken. And a ferret."

"That's a lot of animals, Bella."

"I know! And I can't cope. I've run out of money, but if I don't look after the animals, who will?"

The light from the street lamp blanched her face, drawing all colour from it. Her cheekbones, invisible behind plump cheeks for so many years, were now high and pronounced.

"*Nessun problema.* I told you, I'm here to help."

Bella smiled into his eyes, then stopped.

"But you have your own problems. What about the drinking?"

"I told you, I haven't had a drink for two days. I know it's not going to be easy for either of us, but I want you to help me stop."

"*Nessun problema.*"

"It's a deal then. May I stay? I can sleep on the couch."

"Of course. But I'm afraid it's covered in dog hair. And cages… Perhaps you'd be more comfortable in my parents' room."

Suddenly, it didn't seem so important to keep her parents' room exactly as they'd left it before they took that fateful trip to Italy.

They stood up and Red picked up his holdall. Bella found herself shaking as she opened the front door. For the first time, she was seeing the state of the cottage through somebody else's eyes. The last time Red had been here, the house was clean and tidy, smelling of furniture polish and fresh Italian cooking.

What now lay behind the front door would shock anybody.

Chapter Fifteen

If the stench of dogs, cats and urine shocked Red, he didn't allow himself to show it. Neither did he flinch when Sadie's puppies hurled themselves at him in exuberant welcome.

"Hey! Down guys!"

His eyes darted around, missing nothing. He drank in the broken furniture, the cages, boxes and crates stacked on top of each other, some with occupants that either slept or regarded him with frightened eyes.

"It's bad, isn't it?" said Bella, as she scooped up a passing kitten and hugged it to herself. "I'm afraid these are only some of my cases. There are more in the kitchen and wherever I could find space."

"Yes, I'm not going to lie to you, it's bad. But, like I keep saying, I'm here to help. Now, what needs doing tonight? Tomorrow is a brand new day and I'll have stopped drinking for three whole days. I give you my word, Bella, I'm going to help you sort everything."

That night, Bella slept soundly, and no little boats on turquoise seas sailed into her dreams.

Restoring the cottage to its former self was not going to be easy. Alone in Bella's parents' room, Red made plans for the renovations in an effort to chase away his own demons. He forced himself not to imagine tipping a bottle and watching the contents splash into a glass before raising it to his lips and drinking himself into sweet oblivion. Instead, he thought about mending fences and reglazing windows.

At last, he slept.

It was lucky that Red was so good with his hands. He took over Bella's father's workshop which had remained untouched since his death, with the tools hanging in neat rows and timber stacked in the rafters. Now the sound of hammering and sawing could be heard once more. When Bella heard it, a little ripple of happiness washed through her.

Red's first job was to fence off an enclosure for Sadie's puppies in the backyard which successfully removed them from the overcrowded cottage. Bella brought him out a mug of tea and admired his handiwork.

"Red, may I ask you something?" she asked, looking at him sideways.

"Fire away! Anything."

"I know you said you're going to help me, and I'm really grateful, but what about money? You don't have a job, and neither do I…"

"Ah! There's something I didn't tell you."

Bella raised her eyebrows in question, surprised to see Red smiling.

"You remember that box I made you for your fourteenth birthday?"

"Of course! I still have it."

"Well, do you remember that I invented a kind of engraving tool which I used to write your initials on the lid?"

Bella nodded. Red's eyes were dancing now.

"Well, I patented it, and a big company in Scotland bought the rights to manufacture and sell it. They pay me a percentage of the sales."

"Wow! That's fantastic!"

"I know! And if I invent anything else, they want first

refusal on it."

Bella was still gaping at him when they both heard the doorbell.

"That'll be Auntie Jayne," said Bella. "She said she might pop round. Come with me, she'll be so surprised to see you!"

Red followed as she ran through the house to open the door.

"Morning, Auntie Jayne, I have a surprise for you! Look who's here!" she stepped aside to reveal a grinning Red.

"Hello, Mrs Fairweather."

"Oh my goodness! Red, is that you? I haven't seen you since…" Jayne trailed off, her brow creasing as she attempted to calculate the years.

"Years and years," said Red, shaking her hand. "How are you, Mrs Fairweather? Do you still have the Post Office?"

"I certainly do. Are you here on a visit, Red?"

"Yes, a long one, I hope. If Bella will have me."

Bella's blush told Jayne all she needed to know.

"Will you stay for a cup of tea?" asked Bella. "I've just made some."

"I don't have time for tea, but I'll come in for a moment," said Jayne, entering and catching sight of Red's backyard project through the window. "I see you've made an enclosure for the puppies. That's wonderful!"

Bella nodded reluctantly.

Jayne's mind raced. Perhaps Red would help bring Bella to her senses and succeed where she had failed.

"Bella's place was getting rather cramped with all those pups hurtling around," she said to Red. "Wasn't it, Bella?"

"Well…" Bella started.

Red was a clever young man, and he knew that he and Jayne had a common goal, and that he had an ally in Jayne

Fairweather.

"I promised Bella I'd help sort the animal situation," he said brightly. "I think we'll need to find homes for those pups. Really good homes, of course. In fact they aren't really puppies any more, isn't that right, Bella?"

"Well, no, but…"

"You weren't thinking of keeping all those dogs, were you? I know you'd only consider letting them go to really good homes," he added quickly, before Bella had time to speak.

"I…" she began.

"Mrs Fairweather, do you know of anybody looking for a dog to adopt?" he asked, before Bella had time to say anything else.

"Funnily enough, yes! I do!"

Bella closed her mouth and stared at her friends.

"PC Stan Cooper took a real shine to that pup with a patch over his eye. The scruffy-looking one with hair that sticks up in all directions," said Jayne.

"Good! He'll have a great life at the police house, won't he, Bella? Mrs Fairweather, would you mind asking PC Cooper if he's still interested?"

Bella opened her mouth again, but then snapped it shut, allowing Red to call the shots. Deep inside, she realised she was enjoying having somebody else making decisions for her for a change.

"No problem at all," said Jayne, beaming.

"Poor Bella's had a lot on her plate," said Red. "I intend to help her get things running as smoothly as possible again."

Bella glowed. The pain in her heart caused by the thought of losing Tufty and the other pups and animals was eased a little by the knowledge that Red was there to help her cope.

"Well, I'll be off then," said Jayne. "Welcome back,

Red, it's really good to see you again."

Waving goodbye to the couple, she walked away up the street. A car rounded the corner, swerving briefly to avoid Henrietta who was pecking at something in the gutter.

"I think mending the front fence will be my next job," declared Red, "or Henrietta will end up as flat as an omelette. Incidentally, how did she come to be here?"

"I was at the Drapers' farm, and Henrietta had been attacked by a fox. She was injured and they were going to wring her neck and eat her because she stopped laying eggs. I said I'd treat her injuries then take her back to the farm when she was well."

"Well, she looks very healthy now. Has she started to lay eggs again?"

"Yes." Bella said, hanging her head, knowing what was coming next.

"Don't you think she'd be happier back with her flock?" Red's voice was gentle.

"I suppose so..."

As the weeks rolled by, Jayne was delighted to see big changes taking place. Red replaced the picket fence at the front of the house, and gave the rusty old gate a lick of paint. He varnished the peeling front door and replaced the broken window panes and repainted the frames. He cleared the front garden, removed the rabbit cages and built better ones in the backyard. Best of all, he fixed Don's shed and erected another, so the small animals and wildlife now had new homes outside.

With Bella's reluctant permission, Jayne pinned another notice on the Post Office noticeboard.

Free to Good Homes

Can you give a good home to any of the following animals? We have puppies, kittens, hamsters, guinea pigs, a ferret, white rabbits and rats. Apply within if you are interested.

Thank you!

The response was excellent. PC Stan Cooper had already claimed Tufty and the other pups soon found good homes. Bella shed a tear each time a puppy left with its new owner, but Red's reassuring arm round her shoulders told her she was doing the right thing.

"I'm so proud of you, Bella," he said, and her heart melted.

"And I'm so proud of you, Red. I've lost count of how many days you've gone without a drink."

"It'll be five months soon. It gets a little easier every day."

"I know what you mean. What happened to Mum and Dad hurts a tiny bit less each day. I guess we are all starting new lives. You, me and the animals."

They smiled at each other.

The kittens gradually found new homes, too. One was adopted by the landlord of the Dew Drop Inn, Angus McDonald. He named it Scout, and the kitten fast became a favourite with the regulars.

Another two kittens, with their mother, went to live on the Drapers' farm where they spent their days chasing rats and mice in the barns, or snoozing on the hay bales. The Drapers welcomed the ferret, too, and Henrietta rejoined her flock.

The rabbits and small animals were claimed by village children, each of whom faithfully promised their parents that they'd look after their new pet forever. They probably didn't keep their promises, but Jayne and Bella knew the families well enough to be confident that no pet would ever be neglected.

Even without much formal training, Bella had worked wonders nursing the sick, injured and abandoned wildlife, bringing them back to health. Together, she and Red decided which animals and birds were strong enough to be released.

One evening, they stood together in the field behind the cottage.

"Open the box," said Bella at last, and Red did so.

The barn owl peered around the edge of the box, then waddled a few steps forward.

"Come on, Barney, we're setting you free."

Barney stood tall, lifted his shoulders, then launched himself, flapping on silent wings across the twilit sky to settle on a tree branch, silhouetted black against the pink backdrop.

"You've done a wonderful job with these animals," said Red.

Bella smiled. She was enjoying watching her former patients being set free, knowing they had a natural life ahead of them, and that she'd probably saved their lives.

Mission accomplished, they strolled back to the cottage leaving two trails of down-trodden grass, very close together.

bbbbb

If anybody had asked Christine, she probably wouldn't have been able to explain exactly what kept drawing her back to Sixpenny Cross. Time had blurred Bella's memories of Christine and she rarely thought about her, but Christine's obsession with Bella never waned. Regular clandestine visits to Sixpenny Cross and spying on Bella was like a fix to an addict for her. She craved them, and the overwhelming need to find an opportunity to harm Bella had to be satisfied.

Christine was unaware that she had developed an involuntary spasm. It was subconscious and only occurred when powerful emotions enveloped her. Now, as she sat on the train bound for Yewbridge, the thought of Bella Tait set her eyelid twitching.

bbbbb

Without the cages and hutches squatting in every space, Red could address himself to the task of restoring the house back to how it had looked when Donald and June were alive. He tackled each room in turn, mending furniture or buying new. Bella helped by painting walls and sewing new curtains. She hummed as her needle flew along the hems.

Bella had never looked more lovely. Her olive skin was clear and as soft as thistledown. Her hair gleamed in the lamplight, and her dark eyes were bright and fringed with charcoal lashes unaided by cosmetics.

"Bella?"

Bella looked up.

"Bella… There's something I want to ask you."

Chapter Sixteen

Bella waited, the sewing still on her lap. Red walked over to her and looked into her face, his eyes serious.

"I promised myself I'd wait, not rush things, but... Well, I just don't have the patience."

"Red?"

"You don't have to answer yet, just listen."

"Red, you're scaring me..."

Red knelt in front of her whilst slipping something small out of his pocket.

Bella stopped breathing.

"Bella, I think I loved you from the first day we sat together at school. I can't imagine life without you and I think we are good for each other. I want to look after you forever, have children together, grow old together. I love you, Bella."

Bella gasped.

"Bella, will you marry me? Will you wear this ring on your finger?" Red took her limp hand and straightened the fingers. "It's a sapphire, like your mother's engagement ring, and I used my engraving tool to write something inside. Look!"

Bella read the tiny delicate script. Tears coursed down her cheek.

La mia bella Bella.

"Bella? Do you like it?"

"I love it, Red," she whispered. "And I love you. Of course I'll marry you."

The sewing fell to the floor in a crumpled heap as Red leant down and kissed her passionately for the first time.

Neither of them saw the pale face pressed to the window, flinty eyes boring into the room, one eyelid twitching.

bbbbb

Christine waited her turn in the queue at the ticket kiosk. She'd walked from Sixpenny Cross back to Yewbridge station, and now she'd catch a train home.

Home? Where was home?

London. Nobody would miss her if she didn't go back, but London was where she earned a living dipping into the pockets of unsuspecting commuters. It was where she broke into people's houses to steal their valuables. It was where she squatted in empty houses or slept beneath the arches when she was homeless.

Her mother and father had long since disappeared from her life. For all she knew, they and her sister were still in Yewbridge but it had been years since she had seen them. As for looking for them, that was the last thing on her mind.

She still couldn't believe what she'd seen with her own eyes. Fat Belly Bella *kissing*? Fat Belly with a *ring* on her finger? And where was the fat belly? Gone! Bella looked slender and beautiful, with her almost black, glossy hair cascading down her back.

And who was the man she was kissing? He looked familiar somehow...

Having torn herself away from Bella Tait's window, Christine paid the Post Office a visit. Jayne Fairweather recognised her immediately.

"Christine Dayton, is that you? Long time no see."

"I've been livin' in London," said Christine. "Just came

back to see a few old friends."

Jayne raised her eyebrows a fraction. As far as she knew, Christine had never had any friends in Sixpenny Cross.

"Seen Bella Tait lately?" Christine asked lightly. "I ain't seen 'er for years, 'ow is she?"

"Ah, you probably didn't hear about Bella's parents..."

"What about 'em?"

"It was very sad. They died in a tragic accident abroad."

"Really?"

Christine was surprised. She tried hard not to smirk, then remembered. *So who was that man in Bella's house?*

"So Bella's all alone now?" she said casually.

"Well, not quite. Red Jenkins came back..."

Jayne checked herself but Christine had heard enough. Of course! That's who it was! She remembered Red Jenkins from school, Bella's dorky little pal. His hair was more orange then, and he had been skinnier, but she was certain it was the same Red.

Instead of sympathy, rage consumed Christine. Any good fortune that Bella might enjoy was fuel for the powerful envy that Christine nursed within herself.

How come Bella has a man and is in love, when nobody cares a fig for me? It ain't fair, she thought. *No, it ain't fair at all.*

"Where you goin', miss?" asked the ticket vendor.

"Waterloo station," she replied, jerking herself out of her thoughts.

"Single or return?"

Christine was silent.

"Miss, are you coming back?"

"Nope, I ain't coming back. Well, not yet, anyway."

1978 was an interesting year. Pope Paul VI died, and was replaced by Pope John Paul I, who also died after just 34 days in office. At Wimbledon, Martina Navratilova defeated Chris Evert, and Bjorn Borg was declared the men's champion for the third successive year. Sony introduced the Walkman, the first portable stereo, and the Yorkshire Ripper was being hunted in England.

In June, no church bells rang at Bella and Red's wedding. They'd elected to marry at Yewbridge Registry Office, a quiet affair attended only by the happy couple, Jayne Fairweather and Bella's old teacher from the village school. But it was a joyous day. After the ceremony, Red and Bella posed for photographs in the grounds outside. The air was heavy with the scent of freshly mown grass and roses and Bella's white shoes sank into a fragrant carpet of daisies and clover.

No newlywed couple could have been happier, and nobody could have been more delighted for them than Jayne Fairweather.

Months passed, and the cottage was almost completely restored. Donald and June's old bedroom sported a new carpet, new furniture and Bella had sewn curtains with a matching bedcover. It looked fresh and clean, and she loved it.

Apart from Sadie and Hattie, no animals were housed inside. The remaining birds and animals that still needed Bella's attention were now cared for outside in the shed.

Yes, married life suited both Red and Bella, and as Red began to tinker with more inventions, the future looked rosy.

Christine watched the fields, hedges and farms flash past without really seeing them. She inhaled deeply and blew smoke out of the window.

It's high time I paid Fat Belly another visit.

She crushed her cigarette stub underfoot and sank into her favourite daydream, the one where she poisoned Fat Belly's pasta.

She'd caught the train on a whim, a spur of the moment decision. Train stations and undergrounds were her place of work, where she helped herself to distracted travellers' possessions. She was so skilled and light-fingered, she hardly ever went on burglary jaunts any more, unless she was bored and needed to pump up the adrenalin. When she'd heard the station announcer mention Yewbridge, she'd nipped back to her gloomy little bedsit and stuffed a few clothes in a bag. Then she hopped on board the next train to Yewbridge.

What's Fat Belly doing now? she wondered. *Did she marry that dork, Red? I 'ope they make each other miserable. What's she ever done to deserve 'appiness?*

Christine's eyelid twitched. The mere thought of Bella made jealousy, hatred and revenge course through her veins. She dismissed the fact that Bella had lost her parents in tragic circumstances, and that Bella, in the past, had actually prevented Christine from getting into serious trouble by not telling tales. In fact, it only made matters worse because she resented being in Bella's debt. Christine was deaf and blind to reason.

She had no plan, but she knew Yewbridge was not her final destination. She was drawn to Sixpenny Cross like a fox to a rabbit hole. And Sixpenny Cross was just a short bus ride away from Yewbridge.

From the Post Office, Jayne Fairweather saw Christine alight from the bus and watched her walk up the street to the Dew Drop Inn. She didn't see her come out again.

Christine sat on the bed and smirked to herself. Here she was staying at the Dew Drop, the very place whose kitchen she had robbed continually as a child. Would the landlord have welcomed her so warmly had he known?

She'd eat in the pub lounge later, then maybe, when night fell, she'd go for a little walk...

She was prepared to wait. She lit another cigarette, and amused herself by singeing loose threads along the edge of the blanket.

Chapter Seventeen

Bella pushed her bare feet into her slippers and tiptoed towards the bedroom door, careful not to wake Red.

"Bella?"

"Oh, I'm sorry - did I wake you?"

"No, I just sensed you weren't there. What time is it?"

"Three o'clock. Go back to sleep, I'm just popping down to the shed to feed the baby rabbits."

"Okay, don't be long."

"I won't be, keep the bed warm for me."

She smiled as Red buried his face into the pillow and knew he would be asleep before she reached the foot of the stairs.

Bella didn't need to turn on lights. Faithful Sadie trotted behind her, well used to this nightly vigil and not wanting to be left out.

With a shiver, she crossed the yard, a stiff breeze making her clutch her robe more tightly about her. She entered the shed, closing the door behind herself and Sadie to keep the warmth in. Sadie flopped down as Bella switched on the lamp and drew some milk substitute up in a dropper.

She was looking after two sets of rabbits. One set was almost ready to release into the wild, but the newborns needed her care. Very gently, she plucked the rabbit babies out of their nest and encouraged them to lick the dropper, carefully massaging each afterwards to encourage it to defecate, just as their mother would have done. So engrossed was she that she hardly noticed Sadie sit up and give a low growl.

"Settle down, Sadie. I have three more little rabbits to do, then we're finished and we can go back to bed."

bbbbb

The streets of Sixpenny Cross were deserted as Christine made her way towards Bella's house. She glanced at her watch. Three o'clock. Nothing stirred apart from fallen autumn leaves caught by gusts of wind.

The Dew Drop Inn was silent, both staff and guests in their beds. In her house, Jayne Fairweather had been asleep for hours as she needed to be up to sort the early morning newspapers. She passed the silent police house. Inside, PC Stan Cooper snored in his bed, while Tufty twitched and dreamed on the floor beside him.

Christine smirked. *The police are such idiots.*

She glanced up and down, then pushed open Bella's newly oiled gate and walked silently up the path. She still had no plan, just a terrible need to spy on her enemy and, if she could, cause her harm.

She pressed herself against the wall, merging into the shadows, and peered through the lounge window. She could see nothing inside but automatically tested the window with the tips of her gloved hand. It no longer surprised her that so many people didn't lock their windows at night and, once again, she wasn't disappointed. The window yielded and she quietly pushed it fully open. She paused to consider her options.

Shall I climb in? It'd be easy...

Then she had a better idea.

Reaching through the window, she grabbed a handful of Bella's new curtain and pulled it outside. She inspected the fabric, appreciating its quality before she flicked her cigarette lighter.

Flame met fabric.

At first the curtain only smouldered a little, but then a small flame grew. She watched the fire slowly take hold, the flickering light reflected in her small eyes, bright with excitement, and her thin lips twisted in a smile.

She replaced the curtain but didn't move. She was not a natural arsonist but the growing fire fascinated her. She stared as the yellow flames began to light up the room showing the comfortable and tastefully arranged furnishings. She opened the window a little more, allowing the autumn breeze to fan the flames.

Whoosh!

Now all the curtains were alight and the flames were spreading fast.

It satisfied Christine that she was destroying Bella's possessions. That Bella might be in danger meant nothing, if she died it would be the icing on the cake.

Christine turned away from the house and walked back to the Dew Drop Inn. Once, a pair of headlights approached, but she slunk into the shadows and nobody saw her come or go.

bbbbb

In the shed in the backyard, Bella was finishing off.

"That's the last bunny fed, then," she said as she placed the baby rabbit next to its siblings. "Time for bed, Sadie."

Together they crossed the yard, but as Bella pushed the kitchen door open, Sadie hung back.

"What's the matter, girl?"

Bella smelled the smoke before she saw it. Grey curls were wafting into the kitchen and the orange flicker of flames could be seen beyond.

"Red!" she screamed. "RED! Wake up!"

There was no answer.
No time to lose.
Grabbing a towel from the counter, she quickly wet it and pressed it to her face. She headed for the source of the fire, the living room. Through the thick smoke, Bella saw that two chairs were already on fire and the wallpaper and carpet were smoking. She briefly noted that the living room window was wide open but now was not the time to think about such things. Flames licked the walls and the telephone was now out of reach. Smoke had escaped out of the room and was floating up the stairs.

Bella slammed the door shut and flew up the stairs taking them two at a time.

"RED! FIRE!"

No answer.

The bedroom was already filled with smoke and Red was not moving.

"Red! Wake up! We have to get out! The house is on fire!"

With her free hand, Bella grabbed hold of Red's shoulder but no amount of shaking would wake him.

Bella flung open the bedroom window, lowering the wet cloth to shout an alarm.

"Help! HELP ME! Fire!" she screamed.

She turned back, ever mindful that, at any moment, the fire could block her exit at the bottom of the stairs. Now she needed both hands and so transferred the wet cloth to Red's unconscious face. Coughing, she grabbed him under the armpits and, using all her strength, dragged his inert body out of the bedroom to the top of the stairs.

"Red! You have to wake up! We've got to get out of the house!"

But Red was in another place and her pleas went unheard. The crackling of flames was growing ever louder and smoke continued to seep from under the living room door. Bella knew the flames could explode through the door at any second.

Somehow, she manoeuvered him down the stairs, cruelly bumping his body on every step. At the foot of the stairs the heat was intense. But Bella had reached her limit.

"Don't let him die," she croaked. "Don't let him die."

Coughing and sobbing, she crawled on her hands and knees, up the hall, away from Red's lifeless body, desperate to find help. She didn't get far. Smoke inhalation had taken its deadly toll. Bella slumped, unconscious.

Chapter Eighteen

PC Stan Cooper was so deep in thought that he absentmindedly stirred his tea with his biro. Both Red and Bella Jenkins had nearly lost their lives that night. There was no doubt that they were minutes from death and owed everything to the quick-acting van driver who raised the alarm. The driver had hammered on the door of the police house, raising not only Stan Cooper, but several neighbours.

The van driver arriving just then was nothing short of a miracle, he mused. *If I was a believer, I'd think Mr and Mrs Tait were watching over their daughter that night.*

Somebody phoned the Fire Brigade, while others rushed to the house to find both Bella and Red unconscious. As they were dragged out, the Fire Brigade arrived and took charge. The fire was put out before it could spread.

Outside, Bella gasped fresh air and regained consciousness immediately, but Red took longer. An ambulance arrived from Yewbridge and both were taken away for treatment.

PC Cooper had just finished speaking with Yewbridge Fire Department and their findings were puzzling. Their investigation concluded that the fire at Bella Jenkins' home had begun in the corner of the living room, but no trace of fire accelerant had been found. That made arson seem unlikely. However, there was also no evidence of faulty electrical wiring, or, indeed, any other cause.

So how did the fire start?

Not everybody appreciated that Stan's amiable, clumsy exterior hid a sharp detective brain. Also, having been born in the village, he was familiar with all the residents and privy to many village secrets. His forehead furrowed in thought as he applied himself to the mystery.

Did Red and Bella Jenkins have any enemies?

He knew that Bella Jenkins and Christine Dayton had never been friends, but were they mortal enemies? He couldn't imagine Bella being unkind to anybody, but what about Christine?

Stan cast his mind back to the time when Jayne Fairweather had reported a theft from the till in the Post Office. Mrs Fairweather had thought she'd seen Christine Dayton skulking in the shadows. That same night, somebody stole Bella's bicycle and slashed her father's car tyres. Coincidence? Probably not. He knew Christine had spent time in prison for theft and she was more than capable of slashing tyres.

And then there was that strange incident of Donald Tait's severed brake cable. Had Christine Dayton been behind that? But nobody had seen her in the village at that time, so he'd kept his suspicions to himself.

So what happened the night of the fire?

Two facts kept niggling him. Bella had said that she'd noticed that the lounge window was open. When he questioned her, she didn't remember opening it, and she didn't think Red had either. It was a cold autumn night and they would have kept the windows and curtains closed.

"Was the window locked?" Stan had asked.

"Probably not," Bella had admitted.

The second fact bothered him, too. Was it coincidence that Christine Dayton had been staying at the Dew Drop Inn that very night? Angus McDonald, the landlord, had seen nothing. Neither had any of the guests staying there at the time. Everybody in the village, including Christine

Dayton, had declared they were fast asleep in their beds.

To imagine that Christine had left her warm bed and crept out in the early hours of the morning to set fire to Bella's house seemed highly unlikely.

Or was it?

bbbbb

Jayne Fairweather set the tray on the bedside table, and poured tea into the two awaiting cups. On the rug, Sadie sat up and wagged her tail. Jayne patted her absently then turned to the bed.

"Morning! How are you feeling, my dear?" she asked her guest.

"My throat's still sore, but otherwise not too bad, thanks, Auntie Jayne."

"Here, drink this tea. It'll help. The doctor said to drink plenty of fluids."

Jayne sat on Bella's bed and they sipped their tea, both lost in their own thoughts.

"Just imagine if the newspaper delivery van hadn't driven past just then. And what if the driver hadn't noticed the smoke and flames?" Bella asked for the hundredth time.

"It doesn't bear thinking about," said Jayne, shaking her head. "And if you hadn't been outside, feeding those baby rabbits in the shed, you'd both be..."

Bella shuddered. Death had been close.

"If you're feeling okay, we'll drive over to Yewbridge Hospital and see Red later, shall we?"

"Yes, thank you," said Bella.

"I was talking to Stan Cooper," said Jayne. "He told me that it's still a mystery how the fire started."

"Yes, I know. I'm positive we didn't leave anything electrical on. Maybe it was a loose wire somewhere."

"I'm sure they'll find out eventually." Jayne said, then

remembered something. "Hey, you'll never guess who's staying at the Dew Drop for a few days."

Bella waited.

"Christine Dayton! She can't seem to stay away from Sixpenny Cross, although the Lord only knows why she keeps coming back."

"I haven't seen Christine for years," said Bella. "I wonder what she's been up to?"

*****

Until the house was repaired, Bella and Sadie would be staying with Jayne Fairweather. Thanks to the quick actions of the Fire Brigade, the destruction was limited to the living room, which had been gutted, while the rest of the house suffered from smoke damage.

With Jayne busy at the Post Office, much of Bella's time was spent alone. Red was getting stronger every day and would soon be discharged from hospital, but for now, she had time on her hands.

She made daily visits to the shed in her backyard. The baby rabbits were doing well, and no longer needed their nightly feed. The older rabbits were now six weeks old and ready to be set free.

Bella dusted out the pet carrier, lined it with newspaper and popped the two rabbits inside. She decided that the open fields might not be a safe place to release them, and, leaving Sadie at home, she headed instead for Sixpenny Woods. It was a chilly day, and the track was deserted.

"Bella."

The voice stopped Bella in her tracks.

"Christine, how are you? I haven't seen you in a long time." she said. "I heard you're staying at the Dew Drop."

"Yeah, just for a few days."

"I'm just looking for a spot to let these young rabbits

go, they're big enough to fend for themselves now. Want to join me?"

"Yeah, why not."

Christine fell into step with Bella and the pair of them walked together into the woods.

"So where are you living now?" asked Bella.

"London. I got a great job, pays really well."

"That's good."

"I 'eard about your 'ouse nearly burning down and all," said Christine. "Do they know what 'appened?"

"No, they've no idea what started the fire. My husband, Red, could have died. Well, we both could have. Luckily we were rescued in time and he's going to be all right."

They walked on, and the tree branches met above them, blocking out much of the light.

"Spooky place, this, isn't it?" remarked Christine, her eyelid beginning to flicker. "You could die in 'ere and nobody would find you for ages."

"I'm heading for the clearing by the Wishing Rock," Bella said, ignoring the observation. "That'll be a perfect place to let the rabbits go."

"I used to come 'ere when I was young," Christine said. "I used to carve my name on the tree trunks with my knife. I've always carried a knife. Never know when you might need it. Look, 'ere it is."

Christine's hand darted to her pocket and emerged with a flick knife.

Chapter Nineteen

"That looks dangerous," Bella said nervously. "Put it away."

Christine hesitated for a moment, grinned, then slipped the knife back into her pocket.

When they reached the rock, Bella opened the carrier.

"This spot will do nicely," she said. "Come on, bunnies, I'm setting you free."

The two young rabbits sat on their haunches for a few seconds, testing the air with twitching noses. Then they bounded away into the thicket, white tails bobbing.

"I've been meaning to climb the Wishing Rock," said Bella. "I know it's probably a lot of superstitious nonsense, but my parents always said they believed it had special powers."

She looked directly at Christine for the first time.

"Do you fancy climbing the rock for old time's sake?"

"Yeah, okay."

Bella took the lead. She tugged at the ivy on the rock, testing it. Her toe found a foothold, and she began to climb. Christine scrambled up behind her. It wasn't an easy climb and neither young woman spoke as she concentrated on where next to place her hands and feet. Christine was quick and light, but Bella was stronger. At last they were both at the top, sitting side by side on the narrow outcrop, just like Donald and June Tait had done more than twenty years before.

Bella brushed the dirt from her hands.

"So here we are," she said brightly. "On top of the Wishing Rock."

For a while, they sat together, side by side, neither girl speaking. Bella was the first to break the silence. She took a deep breath.

"Christine, I know how the fire started in my house. I saw you that night."

Christine was caught off guard. Her head jerked round to face Bella, her eyes full of hatred.

"So what? You can't prove it!"

It was at that moment that Bella knew, without a shadow of a doubt, that Christine was responsible.

"Actually I didn't see you, Christine, I guessed. But now I *know* it was you."

Christine's hand flashed towards the knife in her pocket, but Bella was faster. She grabbed Christine's bony wrist, preventing her from reaching the weapon.

"Let go! You're hurting me!"

"That knife isn't going to help you now, Christine. You set fire to my house, and you nearly killed Red. I'll *never* forgive you for that. I've always thought you had something to do with my dad's accident, that brake cable in his car didn't cut itself. In fact, nearly every bad thing that has ever happened to me was caused by you. Let me see… My bike going missing, I bet that was you."

Christine tried again to pull free, but could not escape Bella's powerful grip.

"I bet you loved hearing about my parents' death, didn't you? But still you wouldn't leave me alone. You've stalked me for as long as I can remember. But it stops now."

Christine glared at her.

"I felt sorry for you when I was little," Bella continued. "I tried to help you, but it never made any difference. You hated me whatever I did. And you know what? I bet I know what you're wishing right now. You're wishing you'd never climbed this rock with me, aren't you?"

"Let go! You're gonna make us both fall off the bloody rock!" Christine hissed.

It was the last sentence she ever uttered.

"Not me," said Bella. "You."

One sharp push was all it took. Christine fell, and her head struck a rocky outcrop on the way down. She hit the ground with a dull thud and lay still, a trickle of blood seeping from her ear.

It was a full two minutes before Bella could even move.

What have I done?

She was terrified at what she'd see at the bottom and her legs shook uncontrollably as she clambered down the rock. Christine's lifeless corpse was heaped on the ground, one hand clutching an ivy tendril she had grabbed on her way down in a futile attempt to break the fall. Sightless eyes stared at nothing.

Bella stumbled out of the woods and back to the village. Instead of heading for Jayne's, she staggered to the police house and knocked on the door. Stan opened it. Tufty recognised her and hurled himself at her.

"Ah, Mrs Jenkins," said Stan, his mouth full of sandwich. "Excuse me, just having a snack."

"That's okay," said Bella, uncharacteristically ignoring the dog's welcome. Her face was pale and she held onto the door jamb for support. "I've just come from the woods. I… I think I've killed Christine Dayton."

Stan acted quickly. He guided Bella by the elbow, steering her inside.

"Mrs Jenkins, come in and sit down. When you're ready, you can tell me what's happened."

Bella sank into the chair he offered and sat silently staring at her feet for a long time. Then she spoke. There was no expression in her voice.

"I was going to Sixpenny Woods to set some young rabbits free, and I met up with Christine. I suggested we climb the Wishing Rock, for old time's sake, and so we did. When we were at the top, I pushed her. She fell, and I heard her head hit the rock on the way down."

PC Cooper stared at her, then grabbed his helmet from the rack.

"Are you sure she was dead?"

Bella nodded dumbly, her eyes devoid of expression.

Stan's mind raced.

"Mrs Jenkins, I need you to do something for me. I need you to stay here and don't move until I get back. Can you do that?"

Bella nodded again.

"I'll wait," she said, her hand on Tufty's head.

Stan leaned his bicycle against a tree and hurried to the Wishing Rock. A few autumn leaves had already settled on the body on the ground. He noted Bella's abandoned pet carrier set down close by.

It wasn't necessary, but duty made him lift Christine's wrist and check for a pulse. There was none. Without disturbing any possible evidence, he checked her pockets, finding nothing but a pack of cigarettes, a lighter, a flick knife and a train ticket stub.

He didn't hurry. He sat down on a tree stump and removed his policeman's helmet. A squirrel ran up a nearby tree, its tail twitching as though annoyed by the policeman's presence. But Stan didn't see it. As he cradled his helmet in his hands, he was thinking hard. He stayed in that position for a long time before he finally stood, replaced his helmet and picked up the pet carrier. With a last glance at the body, he marched over to his bicycle and climbed back on. Steering wasn't easy with the pet carrier held in one hand, but Stan wobbled his way back home without mishap.

*****

Stan hung his helmet back on the rack and turned to face Bella in the chair. Her face was tear-streaked and almost as white as the corpse lying in the woods.

"Did you find her?"

"I did."

"Are you going to arrest me now?"

"No, Mrs Jenkins, I'm not."

Bella looked at him.

"Why not?" she whispered.

He sat down in the chair facing her and leaned forward, speaking quietly and deliberately.

"Here's what I think, Mrs Jenkins, and I don't want you to say anything. You see, I think I know what happened today. I've suspected it for a long time, but of course I had no proof. Christine Dayton was always jealous of you, wasn't she?"

Bella opened her mouth but Stan raised his palm.

"No need to answer, Mrs Jenkins. I think Christine was behind that business when your father's brake cable was cut, am I right? Don't answer… And she stole your bicycle, didn't she? I expect she carried out countless nasty deeds, but you never reported her. But then she went too far. Christine Dayton set fire to your house, Mrs Jenkins, didn't she?"

Bella buried her face in her hands. She was sobbing.

"I thought so," he said gently. "Today, as the pair of you sat on the top of the Wishing Rock, she told you what she'd done."

"She could have killed Red," Bella moaned. "I was so

furious, I pushed her!"

"Now here's what I'm going to do," said Stan, ignoring her outburst. "I'm going to file a report. It will state that you were in the woods releasing young rabbits and found Christine dead at the bottom of the Wishing Rock, and that's all. It's obvious that she climbed the rock and fell from the top."

"But why would you do that?" Bella stammered through her tears.

"Because, Mrs Jenkins, if you hadn't pushed her, I believe she would have killed you. The world is probably a better place without Christine Dayton and what's done is done and can't be undone. That's my final word. I don't think we ever need to talk about what happened today again, Mrs Jenkins."

Chapter Twenty

The people at the Fire Brigade carried out numerous tests, little one, but they never discovered the cause of the fire at Bella's house. Most people believed it must have been some kind of electrical fault.

Christine Dayton was dead, and the coroner declared it 'death by misadventure'. She was given a council funeral in Yewbridge. They couldn't trace her parents, or her older sister, Mary. Only four people attended the funeral, and I don't believe they did it out of any fondness for Christine.

PC Stan Cooper, Bella, Red, and my very good friend, Jayne Fairweather, listened as the priest said a few words and the coffin disappeared behind the curtains to be cremated.

Red was lucky the smoke inhalation hadn't done his lungs any permanent damage. He became a very respected inventor and earned a good living. The couple were able to rent a little house with a garden in Bristol where they stayed while Bella continued her studies at the university. Of course Sadie went with them. Hattie had passed away peacefully from old age a few months before.

When Bella qualified as a veterinary surgeon, she joined the team at the Animal Hospital in Yewbridge, the same one that had saved Hattie so many years before.

I'm pleased to say that Red stayed sober. Bella occasionally popped into the Dew Drop Inn, but only to stroke Scout, the cat that Angus McDonald had adopted from her.

As Scout lay on his back enjoying a tummy rub, two figures sat beside the fire, engrossed in a game of dominoes. They were regulars, almost part of the pub's fixtures and fittings.

They were known as the Captain and Sixpence, and the next time I watch over you, little one, I'll tell you their story.

Yes, *C is for the Captain*, but the story of the Captain and Sixpence isn't a pretty tale, my dear, so I'll wait until you're fast asleep before I begin.

If you enjoyed this Sixpenny Cross story,
I'd be so grateful if you left a short review.
Thank you!

June Tait's Cinnamon Hazelnut Biscotti

¾ cup butter
1 cup white sugar
2 eggs
1½ teaspoons vanilla extract
2½ cups all-purpose flour
1 teaspoon ground cinnamon
¾ teaspoon baking powder
½ teaspoon salt
1 cup of roughly chopped hazelnuts

- Preheat oven to 175°C or 350°F. Grease a cookie sheet or line with parchment paper.
- In a medium bowl, cream together butter and sugar until light and fluffy.
- Beat in eggs and vanilla.
- Sift together the flour, cinnamon, baking powder, and salt; mix into the egg mixture.
- Stir in the hazelnuts.
- Shape dough into two equal logs approximately 30cm or 12 inches long. Place logs on baking sheet, and flatten out to about ½ inch thickness.
- Bake for about 30 minutes in preheated oven, or until the edges are golden and the centre is firm.
- Remove from oven to cool.
- When the loaves are cool enough to handle, use a serrated knife to slice the loaves diagonally into ½ inch thick slices.
- Return the slices to the baking sheet.
- Bake for an additional 10 minutes, turning over once.
- Cool completely, and store in an airtight container at room temperature.

Recipe inspired by AllRecipes

Also by Victoria Twead

Fiction: The Sixpenny Cross Series

A is for Abigail by Victoria Twead
B is for Bella by Victoria Twead
C is for the Captain by Victoria Twead
D - Z (works in progress) by Victoria Twead

Memoirs: The Old Fools Series

Chickens, Mules and Two Old Fools by Victoria Twead
(Wall Street Journal Top 10 bestseller)

Two Old Fools ~ Olé! by Victoria Twead

Two Old Fools on a Camel by Victoria Twead
(Thrice New York Times bestseller)

Two Old Fools in Spain Again by Victoria Twead
One Young Fool in Dorset by Victoria Twead

Non-Fiction
How to Write a Bestselling Memoir by Victoria Twead
Mouth-Watering Spanish Recipes by Victoria Twead

Children's Books
Morgan and the Martians by Victoria Twead

Other Ant Press Titles
Midwife - A Calling
by Peggy Vincent

Into Africa with 3 Kids, 13 Crates and a Husband
by Ann Patras

More Into Africa with 3 Kids, some Dogs and a Husband by Ann Patras

Fat Dogs and French Estates ~ Part I
by Beth Haslam

Fat Dogs and French Estates ~ Part II
by Beth Haslam

Simon Ships Out: How One Brave, Stray Cat Became a Worldwide Hero
by Jacky Donovan

Smoky: How a Tiny Yorkshire Terrier Became a World War II American Army Hero, Therapy Dog and Hollywood Star
by Jacky Donovan

Instant Whips and Dream Toppings: A True-Life Dom Rom Com
by Jacky Donovan

Heartprints of Africa: A Family's Story of Faith, Love, Adventure, and Turmoil
by Cinda Adams Brooks

How not to be a Soldier: My Antics in the British Army
by Lorna McCann

Moment of Surrender: My Journey Through Prescription Drug Addiction to Hope and Renewal
by Pj Laube

Secondhand Scotch by Cathy Curran

Serving is a Pilgrimage by John Basham

Fiction

Parched by Andrew C Branham

Children's Books

Seacat Simon: The Little Cat Who Became a Big Hero
by Jacky Donovan

The Rise of Agnil
by Susan Navas (Agnil's World 1)

Agnil and the Wizard's Orb
by Susan Navas (Agnil's World 2)

Agnil and the Tree Spirits
by Susan Navas (Agnil's World 3)

Agnil and the Centaur's Secret
by Susan Navas (Agnil's World 4)

Chickens, Mules and Two Old Fools
Victoria Twead's memoir

Wall Street Journal Top 10 bestseller

If Joe and Vicky had known what relocating to a tiny mountain village in Andalucía would REALLY be like, they might have hesitated...

They have no idea of the culture shock in store. No idea they'll become reluctant chicken farmers and own the most dangerous cockerel in Spain. No idea they'll help capture a vulture or be rescued by a mule.

Will they stay, or return to the relative sanity of England?

Includes Spanish recipes donated by the village ladies.

Contact the Author and Links

Email: TopHen@VictoriaTwead.com
(emails welcome)

Facebook: https://www.facebook.com/VictoriaTwead
(friend requests welcome)

Website: www.VictoriaTwead.com

Free Stuff and Village Updates newsletter
http://www.victoriatwead.com/Free-Stuff/

Twitter: @VictoriaTwead

Printed in Poland
by Amazon Fulfillment
Poland Sp. z o.o., Wrocław